THE GAMER

COLIN R PARSONS

Crystal Peake Publisher

www.crystalpeake.co.uk

First edition published in October 2020 by Crystal Peake Publisher

Hardback I S B N 978-1-912948-22-2
Print I S B N 978-1-912948-20-8
eBook I S B N 978-1-912948-21-5

A catalogue copy of this book is available from the British Library.

Typeset by Crystal Peake Publisher
Cover designed by T K Palad

Visit www.crystalpeake.co.uk for any further information.

THE GAMER

COLIN R PARSONS

Otherbooks by Colin R. Parsons

Wizards' Kingdom
The Obelisk of Ashmar
Jarrak's Darkness (trilogy).
The Curious World of Shelley Vendor
The Curious World of Katie Hinge (2 book set).
Crank Tech One: DESTRUCTION
IU-137
House of Darke
D.I.S.C. Direct-Interface-Shadow-Control
Ghosted
Wizards' Exile
The Man with the Black Shoebox and Other Strange Stories

Contents

Chapter 1: Conflict

The wind whizzed past his ears as he sped across the narrow back streets and alleyways. Had he lost them? He didn't know but he couldn't hear the shouts anymore and that was a relief. Drake found a gap in the wall to his right and slipped into it with urgency. He flattened himself hard against the brick surface, clenched his eyes shut and tried not to breathe. He was sweating and trembling in unison. Trying to hold your breath and breathe at the same time is difficult. His chest expanded and contracted as he gasped for breath, but he hardly uttered a sound. His heart felt like a caged animal trying to escape. He swallowed hard and licked his dry lips; they felt like two strips of plastic. Hiding there a while, he could smell the stale stench of urine, and when he opened his eyes, he could see glistening, broken glass at his feet. He didn't want to stay here any longer than he had to. He waited and listened. It was almost quiet, except for the rattle and tinkle of metal in the background. Someone was working on a vehicle; he recognised the sounds. Besides that, the only other faint noise was that of a dog barking, some distance away. He was safe, for now! The stink soon became overpowering, and he knew he had to get out of there.

Drake nervously tilted his head to peer around the edge of the brick, it was clear; he felt a small sigh deep in the pit of his stomach. He hung on for a few more excruciating moments just to make sure. He puffed out a mouthful of air and was ready.

'OK, time to go,' he said softly and tentatively eased himself back on to the street. Drake scoured the area for any danger and smiled that confident grin. He moved across the last couple of streets and was home in minutes. He sneaked into his house-quietly turning the key in the lock-his eyes creasing and teeth grinding at every click and squeak. Drake then stealthily climbed the stairs to his room and collapsed on his bed. He had only been lying there for five minutes or so when he heard his mother shouting from the bottom of the stairs. He growled in annoyance from the pit of his throat and sniffed.

'Alright, I'll be down in a minute,' he groaned and sat up before he made his way downstairs and into the living room.

It was going to be another one of those arguments again, that Drake was used to and sick of. He stood, head bowed and a little ashamed. He knew what was coming.

'Come on Drake, you know how this works,' his mother continued, 'you can't keep wagging school. Things are difficult enough without adding to them. You knew you'd get caught, right?' She stood clasping the damning letter that the school had sent that morning; truancy being the main theme. If he'd only known it was coming that day, he'd have hidden it before his mother had suspected and everything would have been fine, for now.

'But I hate it there, they all think I'm a freak,' he protested. 'It's horrible. I hate it here too. Why couldn't we stay where we were? Everything has changed and I hate everything,' he repeated.

'You just need time to adjust, that's all. Things will settle down eventually, Drake. Huntsville can be a nice place if you'd just let it. It used to have a funfair at one time but now it has a great new shopping centre. I was brought up here,' she said, trying to smooth over the conversation. 'Ever since your dad…' Drake didn't want to hear anymore and turned away to walk out of the room. His mother bit back hard and shouted at him. 'Don't walk away from me young man,' Her tone changed from soft to grating and he knew she'd turned serious. He stopped and clenched his eyes shut, holding back the tears. He loved his dad. Why did he have to die? He felt remorse and anger in equal measures. What had he done so wrong that his father was taken away from him? He loved his mum too but couldn't handle the situation. He felt a stab of guilt and realised how hard it was for her too. Drake sucked in a mouthful of air and composed himself. He turned slowly and lifted his head to look into her glistening eyes. Just seeing her upset choked him up. He opened his mouth to speak, but nothing came out. Then it all just poured out.

'I'm so sorry mum.' He could barely get the words out without becoming a snotty mess. He tried not to, but it was hopeless. She saw the weakness inside him, and the waterfall of emotion was too much. They clamped together like magnets; it was a hug that the world couldn't separate. He sobbed as she silently streamed tears.

'I'll try, honestly mum I will,' he said, his muffled bleating barely audible.

'I know you will, we just have to make the best of it. Dad would want that, and you are a bright boy. You can do anything. Didn't dad used to say that?' This didn't help matters, and Drake buried himself deeper into his mother's chest and sobbed even more. It was the first time he'd shown emotion since his father's passing. He knew that once the cork was out of the bottle, there was no stopping it. They eventually released each other, and both looked reddened and drained from the emotional exchange. Drake urgently wiped away the snot and tears with the sleeve of his shirt. This was something he'd done since he was a little boy.

'We do have tissues you know,' his mother's shaky voice was almost a whisper as she half-sobbed and giggled at the same time. She grabbed two from the box on the coffee table and mopped away the remains of the moment. Then she reminded herself of the life they once had. The void in her heart just couldn't be filled. She knew this new life for Drake would take a lot of working out.

Drake wasn't used to living a normal existence in a normal house on an estate, he'd always moved from army base to army base. He'd had so many different tutors in different countries; Germany, Italy, Spain and many others. Drake seemed to enjoy moving around the world. It suited him. He wanted to be the same as his father. His dad was a captain in the Army and well respected. One dark day, only a message returned from the battlefield. He'd died fighting for his country; Killed in Action it read. This left a gaping hole in both his and his mother's lives. She was confronted with a severance pay plus insurance and a lot of extra responsibility. The army had always provided for them, but with Drake's father gone, she had to leave the army life and set up a new home. The next step was sending Drake to a new school. They would have to stay in one house, which was proving difficult. Drake felt like he didn't fit in with his new surroundings. His mother came out of her thoughts and back to reality when Drake spoke.

'I'm going out mum,' he said, composing himself. He quickly grabbed his jacket. She'd barely had time to take a breath.

'Where are you going?' she asked.

'Just out, see you later,' he called back.

'Dinner's at six don't be…' But she could already hear the front door slam shut. She took a deep breath and a couple more tears streamed down her face. Mrs Banks hurriedly wiped her cheeks with her hand. She walked over to the mantlepiece and picked up a picture of the three of them. They were smiling, especially Drake, but that was a different life and things would never be the same.

Drake walked along the path and stood at the gate for a moment. He rested his hands on the rusty wrought iron frame. He closed his eyes and took a breath as an April breeze gently caressed his face; it felt good. He lifted his hand and raked away the black unkempt locks from his green eyes; he needed a haircut. A haircut though was the least of his problems. The flash of that letter clouded his thoughts again. He had to make a good impression, if only for his mum. Well, it's the weekend, he thought, as he reasserted his priorities. School was a distant memory, at least until Monday. Hopefully, those goons who were chasing him were long gone. A genuine smile lifted his spirits when thinking of where he was headed. It was the only thing in his life that did put a smile on his normally sullen features. So, he flicked up the latch, pulled the screaming gate towards him and stepped into the street.

Chapter 2: The Arcade

Drake took his time to walk to town, suspiciously checking to make sure he wasn't being followed. He didn't need to worry. The distance was only a matter of ten to fifteen minutes and this gave him more time to think. Drake's mind was still awash with all the sad thoughts and feelings that plagued him. He loved his mother deeply, and besides his Gramps and Nan, she was all he had now. He had to man up and take responsibility for his actions. He was, after all, the man of the family now, at the ripe old age of twelve. It was daunting, to say the least, but he knew he had to do it. This gave him a bit more positivity and zip to his stride.

There was a gaming arcade in town. He'd found it one day when he'd stormed out of the house in one of his strops. It was an old place that had seen better days. There was a shabby front door, which had more scratches than a Wolverine victim. And inside was still set in the style of when it opened. The brown and orange patterned carpet was badly worn from a million footprints, and the surface was speckled with shiny spots of ground-in and flattened chewing gum. The whole place smelled of damp, sweat and popcorn. But none of that mattered to Drake; all he cared about were the games. He loved the sound of the place with all the pings, dings and flashing lights. It had character as far as he was concerned, and he liked it. It felt like a place of sanctuary-a haven for gamers. Drake could breathe and enjoy his time there and get away from all the problems back at home.

Further up the road, there was a bright and sparkly new gaming complex in the shape of The Hills Shopping Mall. To his delight, all the kids went there now, and he could play to his heart's content in the old place. There were classic games on offer and when something new came out, they'd have that too. Bonus! There was never much of a wait to try out something new either. It was heaven.

Drake dipped into his pocket as he walked along the busy street and grabbed the half-empty packet of M&M's he'd bought the previous day. He loved sweets almost as much as he enjoyed gaming. While he crunched away, every bite vibrated inside his head like a mini Earthquake. Drake slowly entered the bottom end of town and after walking a short distance, he approached the first of the shops. It was warm, and he wished he'd left his jacket behind.

He gazed into the Barber Shop at the beginning of the high street. He shaded his eyes with his right hand from the reflection of the glass and stared in the window. A semi-bald guy was sitting in the barber's chair. He appeared to be in his seventies, but to Drake, anyone over thirty was old. He was having what hair he had left trimmed and groomed by the skill of the barber. The youngster chuckled to himself and shook his head in disbelief-what was the point? Drake raked his fingers through his mop of black, shaggy hair and hoped he'd never end up like that guy. He continued on his way into town. He strolled by a hairdresser's–they seemed to pop up everywhere. There was also a beauty parlour, charity shops, a nail bar and a tanning salon. 'Why do women need all this beauty stuff?' He huffed, 'Waste of time if you ask me,' he mumbled under his breath.

The gaming arcade wasn't too far up the road from there. It was only a few metres. Then he saw Lucy Jones! She was making her way towards him and he felt his stomach tighten up in a knot. He took a few deep, panicky breaths. Why was it that when he got close to her–he always fell apart? His mouth always feels as if it was full of cotton wool. He noticed that his heart sped up, and he also found it difficult to breathe. And why did she appear to walk in slow motion, like in a movie? He admitted to himself that he had a bit of a crush on her but didn't know how to handle it and definitely wouldn't let on to anyone else. And what did he know about her? She was in his class and… he felt himself stumbling for information in his head. That was it! That was all he knew about her, except that she was pretty. Her skin and teeth were perfect, and she was petite. He tried not to stare as she walked past. He didn't acknowledge her, and she didn't talk either, but she did give him a muted smile and that was enough. Did she like him? He didn't know, but he wasn't going to do anything about it, anyway. She was bound to have a boyfriend; he was probably one of the goons that were chasing him earlier. Lucy carried on walking and Drake felt like such a fool for not talking… and then the moment was over. He cursed himself for being such a wimp and continued towards the games arcade. He finished the rest of his sweets and threw the wrapper into the already overflowing rubbish bin outside the shop. He had to shut down his overflowing mind. Between his mother's nagging and the feelings he felt for the girl in his class, he knew he had to wind down.

He pushed open the door, and it screeched loudly on its hinges. Luckily though, there were only a few ardent gamer nerds inside, so the noise from each console swallowed up his loud, dramatic entrance. No one noticed him swan in–no one cared to be honest. He made his way down the aisle and headed towards his usual arcade game. He hoped that no one else was playing on it and as luck would have it, there wasn't. A wry smile lifted his troubled face. At last something was going his way. Drake dug deep into his pocket and fished out some loose change as he walked. He was busily fingering the coins, looking for the right money. When he looked up, he realised that he was standing by the wrong gaming machine. He was disorientated for a moment and felt a little stupid. In all the confusing sounds of the arcade, he'd walked straight past his usual slot. Drake looked over to his usual game, but this one was pulling at him like a magnet.

The strange thing was that he didn't recognise this game at all. He looked at the title. The words DEATH TRAP appeared in big, bold letters.

'Death Trap? What kind of game is it?' a thrill of excitement vibrated his stomach and brought a wicked look to his eye.

'Mike, how long has this game been here?' Drake called out to the owner at the counter, but it was too loud inside for anyone to hear him. The owner, Mike Bevan, was too busy reading this month's edition of Gamer's Monthly to hear or want to hear anyone. Drake stared at the screen again. This game wasn't here the last time he visited. The number of times he'd spent in here, he surely would have noticed it.

He was in two minds! Should he go and play his usual game or try this new one? No contest, he loved a challenge. He squinted at the panel and when he couldn't find the coin slot, he was thrilled!

'Where the heck is the money slot?' he mouthed. This brought another huge smile to his face. He looked up and down the panel again and could only find a start button. Surely this can't be free? He pondered. He got excited at the thought of finding something that you didn't have to pay for. This opportunity would only come around once. He read the title again, and there was a bunch of writing underneath.

DEATH TRAP: play the game and things will never be the same. How corny is that? He thought. The button was pulsing away: Start-start-start-start; he felt like it was taunting him. Drake's hand hovered over the luminous red dome. He couldn't believe it–he was sweating and nervously shaking. The excitement was building, and his breathing heightened. He pulled his hand away and wiped a line of perspiration from his upper lip and smeared the excess sweat down the front of his T-shirt. Once again, he placed his hand over the dome, hovering, as if in a shoot-out. He clenched his teeth and tensed his face so tight; it felt like it would break his skin. His chest was heaving as if he'd run a marathon and a wild flicker of wickedness took hold.

He slapped down hard and…

Chapter 3:
01:00:00 Countdown

The sensation he felt was like falling down a deep hole. He tried to call out to the owner as his vision of the game shop faded. A matrix of colour played before his eyes, in the form of distorted, ever-changing bubbles. Each one filled with swirling incandescent rainbows. He was mesmerised momentarily; it was beautiful. But then his lungs began to burn through lack of oxygen, which immediately brought him back to reality. He was underwater! Oh my God, he was underwater! Panic suddenly set in. He urgently needed oxygen and had to get out right now!

Drake exploded through the surface and gagged for a huge intake of breath. He felt the sharp sting of cold air slap his face. He gulped hungrily at the free air, coughing and spluttering excess water from his throat. He splashed about frantically, trying to find something to grab on to. But he was a good swimmer and quickly composed himself. He was treading water when he suddenly noticed the wristwatch (he'd never owned one before). It had a bright, luminous screen which instantly caught his attention. It must be waterproof, otherwise how was it still working? He was confused.

'Where on earth did that come from?' he said, spitting water. He lifted his arm a little closer to his face. The black digits were big and bold on a yellow background. It was a countdown! 00:59:38 was displayed with numbers falling away quickly. There was a small screen located above the clock face that depicted a GPS. The display revealed a flashing amber dot on a white background. The dot was static, probably because he wasn't moving. There were black lines, which mapped out a destination. Is that where I have to go?

'Hold on,' he said, 'Where am I and how the hell did I get here?' Drake closed his eyes and tried to remember the last few minutes before this madness began. 'The game, I was about to play the game-Death Trap,' He remembered. It was coming back to him now. 'I must be *in the game*! How did I get in here?' It didn't matter now; he was here, and that was that. He suddenly felt trapped. 'I've got to get back home. Hello, is there anybody there?' he called out, but his voice was swallowed by the vastness of the water and besides, he couldn't see anyone, anyway. 'I'm alone.' He felt as though he wanted to cry again, as he did earlier with his mother, but fought against the tears.

'This is not helping,' he felt himself saying. Then he remembered why he was there; the watch and the quest that he had to fulfil. He was on some kind of mission. A spark of warmth welled up inside. 'Kind of like James Bond.' A smile pushed away from the homesickness and gave him purpose again. He loved James Bond. For a moment he thought of himself as Daniel Craig. There were others in the game too, he recalled; it was all coming back to him now. There were figures of other people emblazoned all over the console. He must get to the destination before them, and then he can get home again! 'I've got to get to the shore,' he spoke quietly in-between gulps. He swam swiftly across the water. When he got to the bank, he dug his fingers into the soft, wet mud. Drake dragged himself out of the water and onto the shore. He pushed himself up to his knees and felt a little weak, he'd forgotten how swimming drained energy. But he remembered the clock; time was of the essence. He forced himself to a standing position, and felt restricted. He peered at his body in the half-light and understood why-he was wearing a wetsuit. Now, he definitely felt like James Bond. He nodded his head in approval. This meant that within seconds he was completely dry, except for his hair.

He looked around to get his bearings. There in the distance, he saw the outline of a bridge that was lit by a row of streetlights.

'Is that where I have to go?' He urgently looked at his new watch again and it read 00:55:10. 'Wow, five minutes gone already. I have to go,' he said urgently. There were steps nearby, so he jogged towards them. The muddy ground sucked at his footsteps, but the suit was light, which made it easier to run. 'This is amazing,' he said. It felt like a second skin. The mud morphed into deep gravel, which was a lot harder going as each footstep seemed to drain the energy from his body.

Drake groaned but pushed on and as quickly as he could, he made it to the steps. He was now panting as he clambered his way to the top. Once there, he sucked at the air to fill his lungs. He knew time was slipping away and quickly stepped onto the tarmac road. He felt light-headed for a few moments and shrugged it off. The smooth surface was easier to walk on and the short trip to the bridge took seconds. He panted as he rubbed his aching calves. They were sore from the intense exercise. He stood upright and gazed at his wrist to check the GPS to make sure he *was* going the right way. He gave himself a cheery nod accompanied by a grin. Drake craned his neck. The bridge itself was made completely of wood. There were huge beams of timber that stretched to the sky in a complex pattern. He dropped his gaze to the wooden road and the long timbers that spanned the water. Besides the obvious glow of the streetlights and his watch, there was also another larger luminous object. This was situated just beyond the other side of the bridge. He broke into another sprint. As he got closer, the object appeared to be floating, but not on the water–in mid-air!

As he approached, he saw it was a kind of bike but with no wheels. He then remembered he'd seen a movie called Tron; a futuristic adventure set inside a video game. The movie was filled with all kinds of weird and fantastic machines, computer-generated, and this bike fit in with that kind of world.

'I am in a game.' It was really difficult to keep that in mind. He confidently climbed onboard and straddled the body of the machine. Drake gripped the handlebars, but it didn't have the feel of a bicycle at all. This was different. This was more like sitting on a Harley-Davidson motorcycle. For the first time since he'd entered this world, he felt scared.

'What do I do now?' he asked as if an answer would appear somehow. He looked at his watch again and saw that the pip was moving straight ahead. He squinted into the distance, but all he could make out was blackened misshapes that made little sense to him. Drake's eyes were hurting when a visor suddenly lowered over his eyes and made everything look like daylight. He wasn't even aware that he was wearing any headgear.

'What?-This is cool; night vision goggles,' he gushed. 'Like something out of Star Wars,' he said, trying to hold back his excitement. 'This just keeps getting better and better.' He was beginning to realise that he didn't have to force anything in this world. All he had to do was think about it and things would happen. So, piloting this bike would be easy too. He twisted back on the right handle as he'd seen his father do on his motorbike. But to Drake's complete surprise, it shot backwards and crashed into the side of the bridge. Drake went flying off and tumbled onto the wooden floor. The collision winded him for a second.

'Aaargh,' he winced. 'That hurt,' he said as he rubbed his sore bottom and elbow. This wasn't as easy as it was supposed to be. The bike hovered just in front of him like an obedient dog. Drake got back up and dusted himself down; his leg hurt too. He limped over to the bike and had to pull it away from the wooden rail. He noticed there were gouges taken out from the timber and one had snapped completely. He found that it was easy enough to manoeuvre through the air. So, he placed it in the middle of the road with plenty of room on both sides, just in case.

He tentatively climbed back on. He found himself almost strangling the handlebars. He took a deep breath and knew this time to twist anti-clockwise... very gently! He did so and the machine once again surged into life. He was sensible enough this time to apply a slight amount of pressure, so the bike only slid forward. Drake's head still jerked back from the sheer power. He found though, the further he twisted, the faster it went. He also began to work out that if he wanted to go left or right-he just had to tilt his body that way (the same as any bicycle really). By pulling on the handlebar, it eased towards his body and the whole bike lifted into the air. By pushing on the bar, away from his body-the machine dipped. He began to get familiar with the weight transference and was soon ducking and diving as if he'd been riding this thing his whole life. The wind buffeted his face and he could feel the wild locks of his hair flatten against his skull.

'Wow, this is great fun. A real flying machine,' he shouted, and his laughter and excitement echoed. He stopped messing around and slowed down to look at his wristwatch. A sinking feeling hit his stomach; fifteen minutes had already gone while he was playing around. He had to get a move on and find wherever he had to go. There were only three-quarters of an hour to get there. Was he on his own or were there others? He didn't know for sure, but the games console suggested there were others. He pulled the handle into his chest and twisted the handgrip until he sped deep into the sky. Drake had more confidence, and the thrust sucked him back into the seat. He zoomed way off into the distance, following the flashing dot. He could hear the wind whistling past his ears as he focused.

Not too far ahead he could make out luminous patterns below, in a beautiful carpet of coloured lights with criss-cross patterns of luminous roads. A city! I've almost made it, he thought, but he was soon to realise that he wasn't alone. He felt a presence and glanced over his shoulder. To his left and right sides, there were two other flying machines on the same flight path.

'Who are they?' he mumbled. As he said this, his visor flashed with the information he desperately needed; Crystal Moon and Scott Vent-now the race is on. The description of both opponents visualised in front of his eyes. Crystal Moon: twelve years old–brown hair–blue eyes and five feet six inches. Scott Vent: twelve years old–blond hair–brown eyes and five feet eight inches. Their images came complete with the information. These were the other competitors he had to beat to win. Drake twisted the handle to full-throttle and tried to outrun the others, but they were matching his speed. He looked down and saw a series of skyscrapers, luminous and bold. Three stood out from the others. These buildings had flashing rings on top with landing pads. Drake knew they were for them.

He could suddenly feel his vehicle being pulled in the direction of the building to his left. The flying cycle began to steer itself and there was nothing Drake could do about it. All three bikes homed in and landed gently with no noise. All passengers had to dismount from this point. Drake looked across and saw Crystal and Scott glaring back, looking the same as the description on the screen. Drake checked his GPS and saw the dot dancing in the distance, not too far away. The only trouble was that he was on the top of a building, many hundreds of feet above ground level. It would take ages to get to the bottom. He wasn't going to make it after all. But then again, neither were they. He strolled to the edge and eased his head forward until he could see below; it took his breath away. He instantly stepped back. He didn't like heights at the best of times, and it was a long way to the bottom. Drake flicked his gaze over to his opponents and saw Crystal and Scott walking to the edge of their buildings. His mouth dropped open when he saw them simply dive off! He watched them falling and then understood that they weren't falling at all; they were flying!

'This is a game, you moron,' Scott shouted. He could hear the girl laughing as she descended to the drop zone.

'If they can do it, I must be able to do it too.' Drake didn't waste any more time. He took a few steps back, breathed in and closed his eyes. He was shaking uncontrollably and had to push himself.

'I can do this–I can do this,' he repeated. 'It's only a game.' But that didn't take away the fear he felt deep inside. He couldn't let them beat him and opened his eyes. He pushed everything else from his mind and ran forward! He couldn't breathe as he dived off and began falling at a rate of knots. He tried to scream but found he didn't have the power in his body to do anything. Then he saw the ground coming up fast!

Chapter 4:
Frozen

Drake screamed out in terror, realising what he'd just done–he'd jumped off a building! He was wriggling and squirming, trying to find something to grab hold of. But his whimper only lasted a couple of seconds. Soon his rate of descent began to slow down, a great sense of calm dulled the panic. He felt as though he was a human kite, but with more control. His body was cushioned against the wind instead of dropping through it like a stone. He craned his neck and saw the bat-like wings that had somehow appeared under his arms. Forget James Bond–now he was Batman.

He could barely breathe at first, but now the sensation of flying filled him with excitement. He soon found that he was enjoying the experience. It was as if he'd always done this, but how was that possible? The winglets made the descent slower, but it was inevitable that it had to come to an end. The feeling of freedom soon diminished as he came into land and he felt cheated somehow. The landing was easy too. He simply straightened himself up as if he'd just jumped a metre or so and planted his feet firmly on the ground. Drake sucked in a nose full of oxygen and stood upright. He did a quick scan of the area and found himself in the middle of a darkened street and it was deathly quiet. The sound of the wing-flaps, under his arms and between his legs, folding away pulled at his concentration. He lifted his arms and saw there was no evidence that the wings had ever been there. He shook his head in disbelief.

'Cool,' he said smugly. He understood now that anything is possible here. Could he get hurt in this game or was he protected? He didn't know, and he wasn't going to find out the hard way either.

Where was he? He stood perfectly still and peered into the darkness for Crystal and Scott. It was so quiet that the only thing he could hear was his rapid breathing. This was weird. There were no sounds at all. Normally you'd hear a car engine or a dog, or even kids, but there was nothing!

'What's going on? Where are they?' he hissed in a low whisper. He was standing in an ally hidden from the brightly lit main street by bleak shadow. Drake, not knowing what dangers lay ahead, backed up against the nearest wall. This is a game, after all, he thought. He stealthily shuffled along to the end. Slowly and with purposeful movement, he poked out his head to see what was going on. He darted his eyes from left to right, taking in all he could. The road was long and perfectly straight at both ends. There were streetlights regimentally placed all along the endless parade, illuminating any gloomy facades that tried to hide. To his left, there was nothing unusual to catch his attention, but to his right was a different matter.

Now, with the help of his visor, he saw them. They were quite a long way off, but they were there. He zoomed in and recognised the two figures of his competitors, Scott and Crystal. But the strange thing was, they weren't moving. Drake narrowed his eyes; his mind was trying to figure out what was happening. This doesn't feel right, he thought.

'That's weird,' he felt himself mumble. 'They should be way ahead of me by now.' He strained his eyes again to uncover the mystery. The extra zoom facility of his goggles gave him the answer. The two of them were frozen, like a couple of statues!

'Huh. Why is that?' Drake was confused, but there was something else. The two figures were brighter than the actual street lights. They were bathed in some sort of hollow blue glow. Why weren't they moving though? Drake stepped cautiously to the edge of the building. He kept his eyes peeled on the street ahead and then lifted his gaze high above. Whatever had caught them will still be looking for more victims, he assumed.

'They must be trapped in some sort of force field,' he reasoned. 'They were caught out at the same time too.' He gave a little smile. 'They're not as invincible as I thought they'd be. I mean being computer programmes,' he continued talking to himself, 'aren't they supposed to outwit the game they're in?' He shook his head. This was his chance to get in front and take the lead. All he had to do was be more careful than they were. Something was monitoring them and that's how they got caught.

He did another sweep, but this time from left to right. He soon built up the courage to exit the darkness of his lair. He walked out into the brilliance of the streetlights. He felt more vulnerable out here. The stillness of the streets made him nervous, but he couldn't hang around and wait for help. He knew that wouldn't happen. So, he took the initiative and dashed along the pavement towards the two prisoners. Drake kept as close to the shop fronts as possible, trying to blend in. The black colour of his suit made his body almost invisible.

He was impressed by how quietly he could run. He left no echo or slapping of soles on the ground; he was stealth itself. Eventually, he got in range and slowed down his approach. He took one more glance around the area and looked up at the two bodies. They were suspended in mid-air by the shaft of light that imprisoned them. He slipped past, his heart pounding, and kept as close to the darkness as he possibly could. Then he noticed something weird moving above their heads. Drake hadn't noticed it before, and it made him stop and focus. Then he realised what it was. A digital countdown – 49-48-47. They'd been caught out, but only delayed. They weren't out of the game completely as he'd hoped, but they were trapped for now, until the time was up and that was rapidly diminishing.

So far, he was the one trying to catch up, but if he moved quickly enough now, he could be in the lead. He looked above and beyond the digital countdown and saw a beam of light on the roof of one of the buildings, like a searchlight. It was scanning for more victims. Drake had the upper hand and quickly tucked himself away from its focus. The beam floated over without suspicion and continued to sweep across the street. Drake urgently looked up again and saw the numbers were melting away.

35-34-he had to move. The shaft of light was way in the other direction, cutting through the night like a large bread knife. This was his chance to go without being seen. He burst into a sprint and quickly left the others behind. Drake didn't look back to see if the beam had changed direction. He knew that it wouldn't be long before Scott and Crystal were mobile again and he had to get as far in front as he could. He ran for all he was worth and then remembered that he had a mission too. He cursed himself.

Stupidly, with all the confusion, he'd forgotten to check the watch. He looked and saw he was moving in the right direction; it was a welcome relief. Now, following the dot on his GPS, he ran on. Drake could feel the seconds draining away and the gap between his two enemies would soon become smaller. He picked up the pace and felt his heart pounding and his breath pumping like an old steam train. He urged himself to keep going. He tore through the dead streets. It was like running a charity race through a ghost town. The shops were in darkness, and unoccupied stalls littered the town square, ready for market day. Suddenly, his concentration was broken.

'Countdown is now complete. Crystal Moon and Scott Vent, you have nine lives remaining.' The speaker on Drake's wristwatch sounded the alarm. Drake's heart flipped; they were back in the race!

'Oh my God.' He felt like he couldn't breathe.

'Drakey boy, you can't beat us,' The sound of the girl's sweet, melodic voice ground into his brain. 'Give up now if I were you,' she continued.

'Yeah, give it up, Drake. You're no competition for us,

you know that,' That was the cold patronising taunt of Scott Vent. But this game wasn't two against one, it was three against three. There would only be one winner and Drake hoped heart-of-hearts that it would be him. He ground his teeth and sucked in air.

'Come on then, give it your best shot,' he shouted back in retaliation. 'I'm here too and I've already outmanoeuvred the two of you once. I can do it again.' He sped on through the darkness with the two figures hot on his tail.

Chapter 5:
Stuck Fast

They were closing the gap. He could hear them in the distance, their echoed frenzied footsteps sounding nearer by the second. That jolted him to pick up the pace, running hard. He took quick glances at his wrist to keep tabs on his target. It was on the move and getting further away–he felt sick to the stomach, come on–come on he urged. Crystal and Scott were almost on him. They sounded so close that Drake craned his neck to check and… Wallop! Everything stopped. It took a second or two to work out what had happened. He then realised that he couldn't move.

He'd ran straight into a solid object. His first thought was, was he hurt? He noticed that he was still on his feet. Why wasn't he lying on the ground? An impact of that severity, like smashing into a wall for instance, should have knocked him out cold. He was stuck! He tried to get his bearings but noticed that the only part of his body he could move was his head. The surface he was up against was too close to focus properly. He must have thrown his hands up in a reflex action to stop his face from impacting. So, Drake's hands and forearms were locked on. Also, his torso, thighs and knees were glued too. When he moved his head and looked around to take stock, he saw that he was trapped like a fly in a giant spider's web. But it wasn't sticky; in fact, it was more magnetic.

'What is this damn thing?' he cursed. Drake noticed that the web-like material was vast and covered as far as he could see. Suddenly, he could feel a vibration running through the netting. A deep sense of fear shot through him. This felt the same as watching one of those bad horror movies they ran on the telly. Attack of the Giant Spiders or something. He'd always watch part of it and then move onto another channel. But now it wasn't a movie, it was as real as it gets, and he was the victim. To add to this dire situation, he heard the fast approaching footsteps of Crystal and Scott. He knew that they wouldn't help him escape. After all, they were all fighting each other here and with him out of the way, well it would be that much easier for one of them to take the other out.

'Well, well, look what we've got here Scotty. There's an insect stuck in a spider's web,' Crystal mocked. 'How are you doing Drakey?'

'Shut up,' Drake spat back, straining his neck to see them, but it was too difficult.

'Looks like you're not going to make the end of the game Drake,' Scott said with relish. 'All the better for me.'

'Don't you mean us?' Crystal cut in.

'Depends how you look at it I suppose,' Scott replied with a sneer.

'Guys, you're not going to leave me here are you, come on?' Drake pleaded, still trying to wriggle out. 'I thought you wanted a little competition. Or would beating a girl be easier?' He was trying anything to get out of this.

'Who's to say any of you would beat me? Boys, huh, think they're so smart,' she scoffed. Drake could feel the vibration getting stronger. This is the end, he thought.

'In your dreams Crystal, you know I can beat you any day,' Scott said in retaliation. He moved up close to Drake's ear, 'so yeah, I am leaving you here. Have fun,' he snorted. 'Time for me to go Drakey boy,' Scott continued. He looked around for Crystal, but she'd disappeared while he was taunting Drake. 'Where's she gone, the sneaky little-?' He didn't finish what he was saying and dashed after her.

'Don't leave me here you moron,' Drake bellowed in Scott's wake, but he was left alone! The vibrations were intensifying to the point that he could see exactly what was causing them. They weren't spiders as such, but electronic beetles! What were beetles doing on a spider's web? Anything could happen in this world. He stared back. Their black reflective disc-like eyes and razor-sharp molars glinted in the ambient light of the game. Drake hated spiders, cockroaches, beetles, and snakes. These were no exception, only bigger and more threatening than normal. He saw them advance; one-two–three; they were coming from everywhere. He hadn't been this frightened in a long time. He could see that the sharp tips of their front molars were as deadly as swords. But… they weren't advancing as fast as he thought they would-they weren't advancing at all! There were quite a few, and they cornered him off from all angles. Why weren't they attacking? It seemed the logical thing to do, he thought. When an insect traps its prey, it goes in for the kill. So what were they waiting for? It was as if someone had flicked a switch and knocked off the power. Maybe that was it. Maybe Scott or Crystal had found the power point and shut it down. They were helping him, after all. Drake felt a little easier, but that was short-lived!

One of the beetles moved and touched the point of its weapon onto the netting. The second it touched down, an electric shock was sent through the webbing and straight into Drake's body. The pain was so intense that it made his teeth ache.

'Aarrrrrgh,' he screamed–the agony was overwhelming. It felt like a static jolt from a metal handrail, but a hundred times stronger. Drake couldn't let go. He wriggled as best as he could-his breathing quickened, and he could feel his skin prickle. There was a second or so of relief from another burst and he tried to clear his head.

'Stop that!' he shouted at the creatures-he knew it was futile. But all they did was vacantly stare back with their reflective eyes. Drake saw another one move towards the web. Instantly, another bolt of electricity slammed into his body. This time it hurt more than the last one and he knew it was going to get worse. His body was feeling numb, and he was slowly losing consciousness.

'Aaargh, stop that please,' he pleaded. Tears were running from his eyes, and snot was streaming from his nostrils. The insects showed no emotion and more shocks surged through his body. The waves of electricity were intensifying.

'Oow, aargh.' As the pain continued, Drake got weaker

and weaker. He began feeling faint and seeing double. If it hadn't been for the fact that he was tethered, he would have collapsed to the floor by now. His head felt light and he couldn't feel his mouth and tongue. More surges came and bombarded his senses, which made him less resilient. His mouth was more or less numb. 'Sstoop pll-easeee,' he implored them, but the insects didn't. They just continued administering the agony. He drifted off to a different place-the beach with his family. The warm sun beat down and zapped his energy. He lay in the sand, warm and content. A feeling of joy washed over him like a wave from the ocean. Then words filled his head.

'Go to sleep dear,' his mother said while stroking his brow.

'Fight back you idiot!' the voice boomed in his ears as his mother faded away in a mist. 'Don't let them take you. You've got to fight back.' The screeching brought him out of his trance. Was it Crystal? Yeah, it was Crystal! He began to get feeling into his body again. What was she doing here? He shook his head to make sure he wasn't dreaming. What was happening? His focus returned, and he could see some of the insects retreating.

'Why, wha…?' Drake was confused and couldn't speak properly. He looked down to the floor. Some of the beetles were upside down, lifeless. Then, when everything came fully into focus, he realised what was happening. Scott was firing laser blasts from his wrist strap and the enemy was dispersing or falling away; the enemy was retreating. There was less and less adhesive charge to magnetise his body to the strapping. Soon he was able to free each limb and had the use of his body again. Only his chest and stomach were stuck, and he felt someone grab and pull him away completely. Drake fell back with a thump and looked up straight into Crystal's beautiful, deep blue eyes. He was in heaven.

'You all right son?' she mocked and reached down to pull him up. He instinctively lifted his right hand to grip hers and found he couldn't. Drake's entire body was ten times heavier than normal. The electric shocks he'd endured had made him feel like a human jelly.

'Wh-why d-did you com-e back?' Drake slurred when it was easier to talk. He wriggled his tongue and twisted his jaw from side to side. 'You wouldn't want to help me unless I could help you.' He looked at her cynically.

'Yeah, you're right,' Scott interrupted as he blasted the last of the critters away. 'We need three of us to dissolve this mesh,' he spoke bluntly. 'So, get up and give us a hand.' The feeling was slowly coming back to his limbs and Crystal gripped on and pulled him to a sitting position. He felt woozy and had to rest both palms on the ground beside him. He could move, but everything felt numb.

'I knew you wouldn't ha-ve helped me otherwise,' he said slowly. 'You need me.' A smile filled his face to Scott's distaste. He wasn't so sure that Crystal minded.

'All right, enough of the bonding; you gonna help us or not?' Crystal stood expectantly with wide eyes and her hands on her hips. Drake was still in the process of flexing his legs and arms. He was in control of his body once again.

He wriggled his fingers, twisted his feet and bent his knees. He rolled his head from left to right.

'I mean as you asked so nicely, yeah okay,' he replied. He bent over, pushing himself to a standing position. He wavered for a moment but was fine again.

'We need to cover both sensors that give this thing life. We have to break the signal at each end. But we have to do it at exactly the same time. If that happens it will knock the centre probe out,' Scott said, getting straight to the point. 'We need you to go down to that end and I'll sort this end.' Scott pointed to his right. 'Crystal will jump up and hit that flashing dome. If all goes well, that should disable the mesh.' Scott had his head tilted back and raised his index finger, pointing to a red light blinking away high up the webbing.

'Wow, that's high,' Drake reacted.

'Yeah,' Crystal looked at Drake and grinned. 'Too high for boys.'

'Wow, you guys are smug, but you need me, right? So, how smug can you get?' he added with a grin of his own.

'Yeah, yeah. Now have you got the instructions in that little head of yours? We don't want you to mess this up too, do we?' Scott was really beginning to annoy Drake. He peered back at his nemesis and jeered. There was a staring competition.

'All right then you two, let's do this,' Crystal cut in. Drake made his way to the end of the massive beetles' web and Scott went in the opposite direction.

'How am I supposed to know what to do?' Drake asked

himself.

'Because I can hear you dummy; through the comm-and I can instruct you. Haven't you got the hang of this world yet?' Scott's voice danced around inside Drake's mind. Drake gritted his teeth and moved on. He eventually got to where the mesh met the sidewall. There, within reach, was a camera lens.

'All you have to do, little boy, is cover the lens with your hand at the same time as I do. Got it?' Scott bellowed in his ear. Before Drake had a chance to answer, Scott continued. 'We'll do it on 3-2-1. When I get to one, put your hand over the lens to blind your side of the web.'

'Okay,' Drake bit back. God, he hated this guy.

'Ready,' he said as Crystal got into position.

'Ready,' Drake called out.

'3... 2... 1.' Drake covered over his side and Scott did the same. Crystal looked up and saw that the blinking red light wasn't blinking anymore. It was a solid glow. She immediately leapt up towards the centre. She burst from the ground and ascended to within an arm's length. Crystal reached out and slapped her hand down onto the glowing dome and fell back to the ground. The whole network of webbing faded and disappeared, leaving the three of them with no barrier to stop them. Drake ran back to where he'd left the two earlier, but they were gone! So much for friendship, he thought, but he wasn't that surprised. This is a game of survival after all and they were programmes with no emotion. He could just make them out in the distance and broke into a sprint to catch up. You won't get away from me, the words flew through his head. I'm coming after you.

Chapter 6:
Turbo Torpedoes

Beyond the barrier of the beetles web was a different landscape. Gone were the streetlights and shop fronts. Now he was confronted with something he was used to. It seemed familiar to Drake because it depicted rows of what looked like army barracks. These buildings were wooden framed and resembled a network of log cabins. Strangely, there was no obvious lighting here, but there was an ambient source of twilight. Where should he go? Drake was at a loss. Once again as he strained to see, the visor slid silently down over his eyes.

He stood scanning the area, but there was no sign of either of his competitors. He continued searching, sweeping his focus from side to side. It was hopeless... but wait! Something caught his attention and there they were. Crystal and Scott were tiny dots way off in the distance. He checked his watch and twenty minutes had gone by; he knew he'd lost a lot of time at the web. The dot was still pulsing away and moving at a steady pace. Not wasting any more time, Drake took off at a rate of knots. The roads were wide, and he spotted Crystal and Scott in a gap between buildings. He decided that if he cut along a diagonal line rather than zigzagging, maybe he could catch up. He did as instinct taught him.

'I've never run so much in all my life,' he felt himself saying. Drake cut through the buildings and it paid off.

He eventually broke free of the regimentally peppered landscape and was now on open ground. There they were. He felt his stomach churning with excitement; the race was back on again. He came into contact with a network of metal stairs and platforms. This game of Death Trap certainly wasn't dull. Drake took to the nearest stairwell and noisily clambered up to the top. The steel framework moved underfoot and vibrated with every step. Soon he was running along a narrow open corridor, overlooking a dry dock. He could see Scott and Crystal climbing into brightly coloured tubes that resembled life-sized bullets. He had seen something like this before in a movie. Did it resemble a NASA docking port? How on earth was he going to beat these programmes at this game? They were more adept at doing these missions. He had to try though, no matter what. How else was he going to get home? Drake hurriedly descended the last set of steps that led to the waiting launch pad.

He was confronted with a variety of coloured tubes, about three metres long which were set inside a groove in the ground. There were four in all: red, green, yellow and blue. The red and green ones were already departing with Scott and Crystal inside. He could see that Scott, with his blond hair, had picked the red one; his locks visible through the glass-panelled cockpit. He could also see the brown, unkempt and wild hair of Crystal's as she disappeared along the channel after him. They were gone in moments, and he was left standing alone. He needed to catch up immediately before they got too much of a head start.

There was no hesitation with the colours that were left; it had to be the blue one. It was his favourite colour and the closest to him.

The glass roof was already raised invitingly, and he urgently slipped inside. Drake slumped down into the seat. It was extremely comfortable and fitted him snugly. As soon as his bottom hit the base, two straps automatically slipped over his shoulders and clamped him securely into the craft. The roof followed suit and closed, sealing him inside. He was ready to go. But he was immediately faced with an array of lights and digital readouts that appeared on a complicated console. It was daunting, to say the least. He could feel the skin on his face tightening. This always happened when things seemed too difficult, and panic set in.

'Oh my God!' The only time he'd been in a cockpit was at a theme park. The dashboard on those things was only for show. This was real, very real, and Drake felt the stab of fear in his stomach again. What should he do? Besides the digital display, there was also a solid handle lever on a shaft jutting out from the panel. He tried to think.

'It can't be that hard, surely? Come on Drake, you play these games all the time. The only difference is that now, you're actually on the inside instead of on the outside,' he said, sucking in confidence. Throwing logic to the wind, he grabbed the lever. He played with it first and could feel that each side had a twist mechanism. Instinctively he slowly twisted the handle forwards, the same as he'd done on the sky bike. He remembered that twisting the lever back meant that it would reverse. Nothing happened! There was a sound of high-pitched sonic revving, like on his video game Sonic Chase, but no movement in the vehicle itself. What was he doing wrong? He couldn't work it out. The engine was working, or he wouldn't get the revs lifting.

He was getting annoyed with himself. To his dismay, Drake looked through the cockpit window and could see the two coloured bullets disappearing into the grey misty sky.

'Come on-come on, I'm losing them,' he shouted in frustration. He twisted the handle again, with venom this time, as if strangling a snake, but the result was the same. The torpedo just didn't move. Drake lost it big time and banged on the column in temper.

'Why won't you work you crappy thing?' he cursed with rage and a frenzy of blows followed. All the anger of losing his father and the frustration of the school problems with everyone judging him, came out in one enormous explosion. He stopped eventually and sat panting and sweating. He calmed and tried to focus again, but something was annoying him in the background. An aggressive sound.

Bzz-bzz-bzz-bzz-bzz-bzz! The sound gnawed at him, boring into his head. For a second or so he was at a loss, then realisation struck as he looked down onto the panel. There in front of his eyes was a red, flashing button. Brake Engaged. It was pulsing away like crazy, warning him obviously that he couldn't pull away until he released the brake! Drake slapped his head and bit his lip. What an idiot, he thought and smiled at his stupidity. He pressed the button to disengage the braking system and refocused.

'Try this again, shall we?' he said as though he was talking to someone else in the cockpit. He twisted the handle forward. Whoosh! With no brake to hold it back now, the vessel blasted out of its channel like a torpedo launching from a submarine. It took his breath away as he sank back into the seat. This time around, it didn't take as long to manoeuvre the vessel as it did the bike. He soon got to grips with the controls and was flying in hot pursuit after his companions.

'This is mental,' he screamed as the G-Force kicked in and everything around him blurred into a giant smudge. The small ship lifted straight into the sky and whipped along at a rapid pace. A tingle of excitement tickled his insides, and his eyes widened in wonder.

'THIS IS AMAZING!' he bellowed. He looked through the windshield and could just make out the two dots of Crystal and Scott. They weren't that far ahead; if he kept going, maybe he could catch them up. There were obstacles though, and it wasn't going to be easy. He found that if he twisted the left handle, he could change direction from left to right. Twist it forward to veer right and back to veer left. 'Easy Peasy,' he chuckled. Below it was difficult to make anything out, but on the horizon were silhouettes that manifested into a city. There were skyscrapers and bridges, with roads on many different levels–a futuristic city. Drake looked way down into the depths; darkness consumed everything, and for all he knew, it was fraught with danger too.

He found that he had to manoeuvre his vehicle in quick delicate movements, to flit around the many objects fast approaching. He had to slow down to check his watch because it meant taking his eyes away from the navigation window. Drake then realised that on the console was a GPS button, so he pressed it. This gave him the same readout as his wristwatch. So now, he didn't have to look down anymore and could concentrate on the job at hand. He could see his competitors clearly and was gaining on them.

Scott's red shuttle began to pull away when he realised Drake was catching up. How does he know I'm behind him? Drake thought until he saw a small, blank screen to his left. The black monitor had a flashing yellow light below it.

'I wonder what that's for,' He pressed it and a view of the rear of the craft came online. 'That's how he knows I'm coming.' Crystal was only just behind Scott and it became more difficult to keep an eye on both of them. Drake searched the panel for more buttons that could help him. He saw the words Loud Speaker and pressed the domed button next to it. A microphone appeared in front of him. The sound system in his ship crackled to life.

'Turn around and leave this to the big boys,' Scott spoke clearly inside Drake's cockpit.

'You're sounding a bit scared to me,' Drake called back.

'Ease up boys, your testosterone is bubbling over,'

Crystal added. 'Why don't you stop and fight it out like gentlemen?' She was linked in too, and all three were in on the conversation.

'And let you take the glory of winning? No chance, princess,' Scott responded.

'Both of you can look out because I'm coming to get you,' Drake boomed. He was filled with confidence now he knew Scott was rattled.

There were pillars fast approaching and Scott veered to the left in a violent manoeuvre. Crystal had to snap to the right to miss it. Drake couldn't turn, it was too late, so he yanked the handle and stopped dead! The rush of the race faded away like ice quickly evaporating on a hot day.

'Come on Drake, you can do better than this,' he hissed. He was soon back up and running again. The others were gone; he had to find them right now. But where were they?

He sped along, weaving in and out of columns and under bridges, through tunnels left and right. There! There they were. He turned the craft and was soon within ten metres of them. The red and green tubes were criss-crossing and ducking and diving ahead. He zoomed in as fast as he could. He couldn't believe his luck; he was now actually level and fighting for the lead.

Until it all went very wrong! He wasn't concentrating and clipped the edge of a wall that sent him spiralling out of control. The sky and ground became one, and he couldn't reclaim control of his craft. He felt sick and dizzy. He had to straighten up or, well; he didn't know what would happen. He worked hard at the controls and soon had his shuttle back under his control again. He slowed right down and regained the momentum he needed to rejoin the race. There was a humongous bang that shook the buildings around him and vibrated right through his shuttle.

'What the hell was that?' he cursed. He was about twenty or so metres from the ground. He wrestled with the joystick and lifted the shuttle back into the sky. He set his ship to hover in a position high over the city. He could see plumes of smoke rising from between a group of smaller buildings. Drake swooped down and made his way to the site. As he got closer, twisting his way through the confusion of grey, he could see the two vessels that belonged to Scott and Crystal. The green one was grounded, but the red one was aflame.

'What the-?' But he didn't finish his sentence, as an explosion took a whole chunk of the building next to him. He was being fired at. He dipped down towards the ground, and his craft automatically lowered the landing gear. 'Preparing to land,' came a robotic voice from the console and moments later, he landed next to Crystal's ship. He was still under attack and dived out of the cockpit, finding cover in the rubble. For the first time in his life, he knew he was in a game, but in a real war zone too. It didn't feel as much fun as it did playing his war games. He was scared, but his companions needed him, even if they were his enemy. His gaming head kicked in, and Drake was ready to help.

Chapter 7: D.R.O.D.

There were explosions everywhere; dust and debris made it almost impossible to see anything at all. Drake coughed and spluttered as he dug into hiding. He could hear his heart pound against his ribcage, and every thud took his breath away. The back of his throat burned, and his mouth was sandpaper dry. He ran his tongue over his teeth, coating the inside of his cheeks with a smooth layer of saliva. He swallowed hard while he crouched down in the dirt, trying to get his bearings. He rubbed his eyes-blinking as he peered into the grey smoke. He swallowed once more, but his mouth was drying out. What he wouldn't do for a few mouthfuls of water. He suddenly saw something glisten through the dust. It took a moment to try and work out what it was, but when he did, he couldn't believe his eyes. Maybe it was an illusion created by the computer game. He was outside the entrance of an office building, or what was left of it. Just inside the entrance, which was a hole and a pile of rubble now, was a vending machine. One of the explosions had blown it apart, leaving just the mangled outer casing and a massive damp patch. Drake looked on in dismay when a single bottle of water rolled along the ground. It stopped directly by his knee and was intact. He thought he was dreaming.

He looked at it with complete astonishment.

'Okay water bottle,' he said in a hollow voice, 'are you an illusion?'

He dipped his hand down towards the plastic bottle, somehow expecting his fingers to pass through it. It was real! He couldn't believe it. Drake scooped it up and twisted off the cap. He took a small mouthful at first and swilled it around his tongue, cheeks and throat, then spat it out. His father had taught him that if you swallowed and started coughing, the enemy could find your position. He sank a few gulps and took a breath. He wiped his mouth and swigged what was left of the bottle. It tasted so good.

He squinted back at the cloud of dust again. His visor didn't help much either; there was so much confusion that it couldn't pinpoint or focus on anything specific. He kept his head down until he could figure out what to do.

'Crystal, Scott, where are you?' he screamed as the gunfire continued to erupt in the background. Drake tossed the empty bottle to one side and dragged himself over the rubble, keeping his head down. He searched through the deluge. It was almost impossible to focus on the mayhem. The gunfire died down for a while and he could hear coughing somewhere, not too far away.

'Over here.' It took him a while to work out exactly where the voices were coming from. Luckily for him, the lull continued, and this gave way to the smoke thinning in different areas. Drake raised his head slightly and peered through the settling, grey wisps of dust. He could just make out two figures crouched behind a heap of stone rubble and a length of girder. The place was a mess. Besides the tumbled buildings, small fires were breaking out all over too.

'I'm coming over,' he whispered in a high pitch, trying not to shout. Drake slowly eased up to eye level and took a quick scan. The coast looked safe at this point.

'Keep low or it will see you,' Crystal's melodic tone sliced through the mayhem, like a machete hacking fronds in the jungle. Drake dropped onto his belly and slowly crawled along the ground like some kind of human caterpillar. This was crazy. Who was attacking them? It was hard work manoeuvring through the lumps of masonry and wire netting, but he eventually slipped down beside them. He noticed that their jumpsuits were covered in the grey dust. They were all almost completely white, as if someone had emptied a sack of flour over them.

'What's going on?' he questioned in a more audible tone.

'Shhh, we don't want to attract any more attention than we have to. It's DROD,' Crystal said urgently, whilst trying to see through the make-shift barricade. She didn't even look at him when she spoke. Crystal's eyes were fixed ahead.

'DROD?' Drake was confused. 'What's a DROD?'

'DROD,' Scott bit back, his distaste evident. 'Defend, Retaliate, Overcome and Destroy,' he explained, as if Drake should have known already. 'DROD is a multi-weapon defensive system that we need to get past somehow. And it isn't gonna be easy.'

'Sounds impossible,' Drake's off-the-cuff remark came with looks of annoyance from the other two. 'What?'

'Nothing's impossible in Death Trap dummy,' Crystal's

hurtful comment made Drake cringe. God, he hated these know-it-all programmes sometimes.

'So, what do *we* need to do then genius's? If you two are so clever,' he snapped back in anger. He clenched his teeth together, wondering why he'd stopped to help these idiots.

'Oh, good grief. We have to disarm it, don't we?' Scott's condescending tone didn't sit well with Drake.

'Why are you such a jerk, Scott?' Drake hissed; his eyes narrowed.

'Hit a nerve, have I?' Scott chuckled. Drake didn't answer, and they stared each other out.

'Will you two knock it off,' Crystal interjected when she turned and realised what they were doing, 'we have a job to do.'

'All right. How do we disarm it?' Drake responded and folded his arms. He was beginning to resent Crystal, even though he fancied her quite a bit, but he had to remember that she was just a computer programme, like Scott. But, for the first time since he'd met these emotionless beings, he felt good about himself. They had no answer to the problem. 'Well? I thought you would have come up with something BRILLIANT by now.' The sarcasm came thick and fast.

'We're going to have to come up with something fast,' Crystal was a little meeker in her reply this time.

'What do you mean? You two super-intelligent programmes haven't even got a plan?' Drake was loving every moment of this and there was a smile added that was wider than the Grand Canyon. They seemed to be out of answers for once.

'OK, what's its weakness then?' Drake decided to contribute something to the problem at hand. This was the first time he had been allowed to contribute. He looked at them, and after a moment or so, he was amazed at their response; nothing! He'd been playing games long enough to know about battle strategies. He shook his head in disbelief.

'It doesn't have one,' Scott spoke up eventually.

'Everything in this world *and* my world has a weakness,' Drake insisted. 'Nothing is without weakness. We just have to find out what it is.' There was a lot of pondering and silence from all three of them.

'It does have a weakness,' Crystal chirped up. Scott and Drake looked at her in anticipation. 'There is a button mechanism at the back of its domed head which can be switched off.' She'd calculated this in her complex mind. Scott was silent for once.

'There you go then,' Drake replied smartly. 'It's got to reload at some point to, I presume?'

'Reload? No, it has a continuous arsenal,' Crystal said whilst lifting her eyebrow as though everyone should know.

'OK. What's it look like? Can it move?' Drake asked.

'What do you mean, can it move?' Scott was confused. Drake was intrigued. He realised that sometimes computer programmes do get glitches, and he thought Scott was experiencing one right now.

'Is-it-mobile-or-fixed-in-one-place?' Drake spelt the words out as slowly and annoyingly as he possibly could. Scott looked at him with contempt.

'It's guarding the entrance to the next level, and doesn't need to move,' Crystal added, trying to keep this conversation at some kind of normal level.

'Then it's simple, isn't it? We have to split up, get behind it somehow and switch it off,' Drake announced with a massive grin.

'It can detect us, that's the problem, idiot,' Scott retorted.

'There must be a way we can do this. Especially if we distracted it, surely? Let me take a look at this DROD thingy,' Drake looked at Crystal.

'OK, don't go and put your head out so it can see you. Look through here,' she indicated to a gap in the stonework. 'Here, you can see it, but it can't see you.' Drake did as he was told and tentatively peered through the hole. The whole spectacle was revealed to him in immense detail. The smoke situation was still causing a certain amount of blurred vision, but once it cleared, Drake's jaw dropped. DROD was a massive piece of impressive military hardware. It was like nothing he'd ever seen before. He could see the entrance to the next level straight past it, but it would be impossible to get there. The robot itself was situated to the right of the exit and could probably see everything from its tower. The structure reminded Drake of a lighthouse of sorts, except there was no ocean here. The robot was built in the shape of a tower. It was a clever design. It was roughly the size of an average house, about twenty feet high and made of metallic metal panels. The top was exactly as Crystal had described; a shiny dome. The dome had a beam of light at its centre, which sent a shaft of white light over the perimeter. The one advantage they did have was the fact that it was static. But the array of weaponry it held looked daunting. How were they going to outmanoeuvre this thing? He didn't reveal his doubts to the others.

They were right, this wasn't going to be easy. Drake looked around and saw a rock that was the size of a tennis ball. He picked it up and threw it long and hard when the beam of light floated way past them. Immediately as the rock crashed through a window in a nearby building, DROD sprang into action. It spun around in the time it took to blink and sent a blast of laser cannon directly at the building; disintegrating the brickwork into dust. Drake climbed back down, taking cover and looked ominously into their faces.

'Well,' Scott probed. 'Do we just walk up to it and switch it off?' He was grinning now.

'We still need some kind of distraction. I know it's fast, but if it has to cope with a few different actions, that will give us some time,' Drake said while rubbing his chin, something he always did when working out a problem.

'Or, so one of us can get vaporised whilst the other two disconnect DROD?' Crystal glared, 'is that it?'

'Something like that,' Drake pondered and grinned.

'Well, it's not going to be me,' Scott said defiantly.

'Count me out of this stupid plan too,' Crystal added. 'I want to finish this game as much as any of you.'

'It doesn't have to be any of us, that's the point!' Drake insisted. Scott and Crystal looked at him with blank expressions.

'You are not as smart as you make out, you know,' he continued.

'What do you mean?' Scott asked. 'You talk complete rubbish sometimes, Drake.'

'Can those two shuttles be worked remotely?' Drake said, looking at Scott and pointing. Scott looked at his vessel, which was burned out, and at Crystal's that was still in one piece.

'Yeah, well mine is shot, but Crystal's is fine, why?'

'I know yours is totalled, but mine isn't,' Drake pointed over to his. 'If you can work mine and Crystal's, that would be great.'

'We can work both of them from our wrist controls. But what's that going to achieve?' Scott questioned.

'You can control mine without my wrist control too then?' Drake asked.

'Yeah, that's no problem,' Scott said, 'it's only a matter of adjusting the signal.' The two programmes were intrigued.

'OK, that's great. If we can get as close as possible to DROD. Close enough to get at least within a couple of metres; I can hide and make my way to it. I can climb up and hopefully disconnect it. You two can have fun keeping it occupied with the shuttles, undercover. So, you'll have to be pretty sneaky to give me a chance to get there. That isn't a bad plan, is it? I take all the risk and you two get to play with your toys and wait in safety. Or, if you have any different ideas, let me know now,' he said, looking at both of them.

'Why can't I climb up?' Crystal queried.

'Have you got to question everything I say and do, Crystal? Just listen to me for once. The two of you are computer programmes, right?' Drake flipped his eyes from side to side. They reluctantly nodded.

'You will stand more of a chance of controlling and weaving your way through DROD's firepower than I will. You are probably more used to the controls than I am. Dare I say it; your skills could keep it occupied for longer. Until it finally blows you up, of course. This will hopefully give me enough time to do what I have to do.' He waited for some more negative feedback, but there was none. They didn't question him for a moment. 'So it's agreed then?' They nodded. Drake was stunned that they didn't have any comebacks.

'Have I outwitted you?' The sarcasm seeped through again.

'You're a tool sometimes,' Crystal bit back.

'Don't forget Drake, this by no means makes any difference to us as a team now. Because we're not friends and we'll never be. When we–if we get past DROD, then it's back to fighting against each other again.'

'I know,' Drake replied, aware that it would go back to normal later. But for now, they had to work as a team.

'That goes for me too,' Crystal added, but there was a smile connected to that comment. Did he have a chance with this… girl? But once all this was over, she was just software, he was confused. What exactly was he hoping for?

Anyway, they had bigger things to deal with at the moment; this new mission.

Chapter 8:
Fade

DROD was scanning the area for a possible attack. Its wide and threatening spotlight was constantly sweeping the carnage below. The three fugitives were hidden away in the rubble, monitoring the machine's every move. Drake waited and timed the white arm of the spotlight for what was the umpteenth time. The others were getting edgy.

'Are we doing this or what?' Scott complained, his impatience getting the better of him. Drake was facing away from his counterpart. He closed his eyes tightly and bit his lip in annoyance.

'Look, Scott,' Drake said, the bitterness evident in his tone. 'We only get one go at this, so it has to be at the right time, or we've blown our chance,' he said with concern. 'When the beam is at its furthest point, we can crawl closer to DROD and then we'll have a better vantage point,' Drake informed them. He swallowed hard; his throat was dry again.

'We know. We're programmed for this,' Scott quibbled.

Drake turned to face Scott, 'Oh, that's why you were both trapped here in the first place then?' Drake retorted flippantly.

'Okay boys, are we going to do this or argue amongst ourselves?' Crystal interrupted the bristly conversation.

There was silence as Drake and Scott stared each other out. Drake finally broke away first and turned to concentrate on the moving light one more time.

'OK, it's time to go,' Drake hissed urgently.

'Come on, this way.' Crystal was already crawling through the debris. The others followed obediently. It was tough going on the uneven surface. They had to grapple along, making sure they kept their heads down, and then stop; wait for the light to pass over and continue. This went on for an age and they didn't seem to be getting anywhere.

'Geez, this is not easy,' Drake whispered, panting as he pushed on his belly.

'Shut up and man up.' Was all the sympathy he got from Crystal. Scott just smirked to himself and said nothing.

'Hold up,' Crystal grunted, and they stopped behind her. 'There's a clearing here, we'll have to take it in turns. If we go at the same time, DROD will definitely see us.' Drake and Scott knew what Crystal said made sense. All three looked up. The spotlight was doing its usual sweep; when it had passed, Crystal took her chance and lurched forward. She quickly scurried along the ground like some kind of speedy insect and dived behind a pillar, loosening rubble in her hast. She froze as the masonry cracked and bounced down a slope, letting out a series of warnings. Drake held his breath.

Suddenly, the light shaft stopped its routine and instantly made its way back to the source of the sound. It hovered over where the now small wisps of dust were rising and let out two blasts from its cannon. The impacts sent concrete chunks, wood and metal flying in all directions. Drake and Scott cowered down as low as they could and froze. A cloud of dust hovered above their heads and slowly began to disperse. There was a quiet period that could only be described as scary. Drake opened his eyes and couldn't see a thing at first. The white searchlight was still prominent, giving the rising dust a ghostly setting. He looked at Scott and put his finger to his lips, shaking his head. DROD concentrated the light directly over their heads for a few more seconds. But it was distracted by another sound further over and immediately responded. There was still the noise of falling debris as Drake called over to Crystal, fearing the worst.

'Crystal, are you OK?' Drake hissed. There was no reply, which made things worse. God, I hope she's OK, he thought.

'Crystal,' Scott called out this time as quietly as he could without arousing the robot. 'Where are you?'

When they knew it was safe, and the spotlight was out of range, the two of them dashed over the open ground together, abandoning the previous instruction to go single file. The two boys dived by the side of the pillar, but there was no sign of the girl.

'Where the hell is she?' Scott sounded concerned, and that shook Drake, as he thought Scott didn't care about anything.

'She's got to be here somewhere, under the rubble maybe? Come on, dig,' Drake insisted. They scurried around in a frantic bid to find her, whilst trying not to make too much noise. They didn't need DROD's attention right now. Scott suddenly called out.

'Drake, here quickly I can see her hand.' They pulled the loose debris that pinned her down. Soon they found her arm and head. Drake cleared away the rest of the debris as Scott was bringing her round.

'Crystal-Crystal, talk to me,' Scott pleaded. There was no response.

'Crystal, wake up,' Drake was beside her, slapping the back of her hand. This seemed to have the desired effect, and she began regaining consciousness. She coughed and lifted her hands to her face, clearing the dust from her eyelids. The deep blue of her beautiful eyes cut through the chalky white of her complexion.

'Oh, thank God,' Drake gasped. He could see the look of relief on Scott's face.

'Wha-what happened?' she asked.

'Nothing unusual for us,' Scott said with a grin. 'Just the odd war zone.'

'We need to go now. Come on, it's just over there,' Drake added. It was true they were almost to the base of the tower, which was only about ten metres away.

'Did you miss me?' Crystal grinned, taunting Scott by stroking his cheek.

'Don't be stupid,' Scott answered dismissively, 'without you it would have been a bit more difficult that's all.' Drake grinned at Crystal as she got to her knees. She peered back, her eyes dreamy and innocent. She was playing both of them.

'Are we ready to do this?' Drake asked, there were nods all round.

They prepared to move out once more. The three of them waited again for the light to pass over and then stealthily skimmed through the shadows. They found the remains of a wall that made a fantastic cover to work their plan. It was a great vantage point in which they could control the torpedoes without being seen. The three grouped and crouched in silence.

'Right,' Drake spoke up, 'you're going to have to give me enough time to get to the dome and do what I have to do. Do some smart aerial manoeuvres with those small crafts. Keep that robot occupied. Do anything you can so that DROD is completely taken off guard and has to concentrate. The longer you can give me, the easier it will be to try and disconnect it. I know I'm repeating myself, but we only get one shot at this. If this doesn't work, it's game over for all of us,' He sounded serious as he looked around.

'We know what we have to do Drake. Just make sure you complete your end of the bargain,' Scott countered.

'When you get up there Drake,' Crystal informed him, 'just behind its head is a slider control. Push it to the right and a compartment should pop open. Just hit the button and the whole machine should power down,' she said ominously.

'Should power down? You don't sound too convincing, Crystal,' Drake looked worried. 'It will power down, I hope.'

'Well, what she means is, it's never been done before. But we're sure it is there; our onboard intelligence system tells us it is. We can only go off that,' Scott's explanation wasn't convincing either. Drake subconsciously rubbed his forehead, as he always did when he was distressed. He shook his head and let out a huge breath.

'Oh great,' he reacted. 'Well, let's hope you're both right. Are we ready? Then let's go.' Scott and Crystal tapped away on their wrist controls and the green and blue consoles lit up.

'They are responding, great, well that's the first part done,' Scott looked at Crystal and she nodded. Drake edged his way to the rear of the tower until he had no more cover and waited. Crystal and Scott waited for the searchlight to stretch to its furthest point and fired up the shuttles. It didn't take long for DROD to respond to the sudden movement, and soon enough its probing light was dancing over the area–searching!

Both torpedoes burst out of the carnage and shot into the sky. As Scott and Crystal raised the vessels, they manoeuvred them instantly in opposite directions. The laser fire was Drake's cue to dash to the switch. He sprinted towards the robot tower and quickly climbed up on the smooth outer surface. Laser blasts and explosions were in full swing as DROD tried to hone in on the intruders. It was a full-blown war zone with explosions, dust and heavy light beams coming from the tower. Drake could feel the power of DROD with every blast from its cannon. The whole tower shook in vibration and Drake had to make sure he held on tight. The rapid-fire rattled its way through his body and made him feel slightly nauseous, but he shook it off. He knew how important his mission was.

Drake felt as light as a feather as he scrambled up the steel plates that riveted the beasts' outer shell. It was easier than he'd thought. There were plenty of grips to help him ascend. He found himself three quarters of the way up the north side of the fortress when he glimpsed the blue of his shuttle burst into flames. His heart sank. Time was running out.

'One down, one to go,' he mumbled as his fingers clawed at the edge of the robot's shoulder. He was almost there when the second and final target exploded into tiny pieces.

'Oh my God,' he mumbled. Drake's heart quickened. Time was up!

'Well, that's it from our end,' Scott mumbled, searching for Drake's outline. 'That thing should have already powered down by now,' he grimaced.

'It's up to him now,' Crystal added, 'he'll do it.'

Drake shuffled along a ridge and could see it. His heart quickened, and his eyes widened. Right there in front of him was the slider control. A fantastic feeling of relief consumed his thoughts. He smartly pushed the dial to one side, and the compartment slid open. His entire face creased up into a smile when he saw the button. He heard one more blast from the robot's weapons just before he hit the red button, and the beast was instantly silenced. The computer system powered down with huge diminishing sonic sound. DROD, its life force was no more. Drake climbed to the top of the dome and screamed out in victory.

'Yeah, we did it,' His echoed ranting boomed across the city. He scanned through the dust and debris, but he couldn't see Scott or Crystal. Something was wrong!

'Crystal, Scott, where are you?' he shouted.

'Drake, she's been hit. You have to help her,' Scott screamed back at him.

'Hold on, I'm coming down,' Drake screeched.

'No, don't,' Scott called out.

'Why?' Drake was confused. 'Come on, I'll help you,' he insisted.

'You have to get DROD's life chip. It's the only way you can help her now,' Scott persisted. Drake stood on the shoulder of the giant and with his visor could zoom in on Scott's position.

'What life chip? Where is it and why do I have to get it?' Drake questioned.

'Look, we haven't got much time, Drake. She's fading fast and only the life chip will help her. She's been hit by a Drainer missile. That will take all of her lives, so you have to quickly get the life chip into her as soon as possible,' he pleaded and sounded concerned. Why is he helping her? Drake thought. Surely, he wants to get rid of both of us so that he can win the game?

'Where is the life chip, Scott?' Drake shouted again, 'and what does it look like?'

'It should be on its chest plate somewhere. It will look like an orange glowing light. Just touch it and it will open.' Drake quickly made his way down from the shoulder and onto the front of DROD's gigantic chest. There it was, just below the head and glowing away as Scott had said. Drake wasted no more time and touched the button. Exactly as Scott had instructed him, out popped a tray. Drake reached in and lifted out a computer chip about the size of a fifty pence piece. He quickly scaled his way down the front of the tower. When he reached the bottom, he dashed over to where Crystal lay.

'Quickly,' Scott held out his hand and took the hardware from Drake's grasp. Crystal was there only in essence. Even though she was a computer programme, she looked like a ghost to Drake. He could only just make out the outline of her form against the dirt and brick around her. Scott was also in a state of fade. He had his hand on Crystal's stomach and seemed to be lending his life force between the two. Scott reached in and placed the chip inside her stomach cavity. This made the whole thing so real to Drake. They are only computer programmes, he told himself. But sometimes they seem so human.

Immediately she became rejuvenated, and the Crystal Moon unit became whole again. She sat up, fully formed and beautiful. Scott's body slowly became solid too. It was amazing watching the transformation grow from nothing to normal in the blink of an eye.

'We have no lives left now,' Scott admitted. 'The missile took away Crystal's, and I gave mine up helping her.'

THE GAMER

Crystal opened her eyes as if she'd been in a long coma.

'What's the matter with you guys? Is DROD dead?' she asked, oblivious to her near-death experience.

'Yeah, the big beasty is gone,' Drake said. His happiness at seeing her function again was obvious.

'Come on, we have a game to finish then.' And she got straight to her feet as if nothing had happened. Scott looked at Drake and smiled.

'What's the matter with you guys?' she looked confounded.

'Nothing,' the two boys answered in unison.

'You're holding me up. Come on,' she insisted, 'let's get out of here.'

Chapter 9: Storm

All three left the battle-torn DROD area and moved along through to the next part of the game. The entrance was another darkish place, which Drake was getting used to. It was a long tunnel, with yellow emergency lighting spaced sporadically along the centre of the arc above their heads. There was no possible way of knowing what lay ahead. It was also becoming a bit monotonous and Drake withdrew from the others for a brief moment or two. He took a long, silent sigh. Was he ever getting home? These two wanted to end his life and possibly each other's, but he couldn't help but like them now, especially Crystal. The thought of never seeing his mother or grandparents again though made him feel sick. He had to make it out, no matter the cost.

'Crystal,' Scott called after her. He needed to tell her, but for once found it difficult. She stopped and turned to face him, waiting for Scott's response, which didn't happen. Drake stood behind and said nothing. Crystal noticed this and focused her attention on him.

'What's the matter, Drake? You look so serious,' Crystal's face contorted, which made a crease in her forehead. He'd never seen that before. Weren't computer programmes supposed to be perfect at all times? Were these two changing somehow?

'You were just hit by a Drainer!' he said, his brown eyes

deep with concern.

'No, that didn't happen,' she said, tears forming in hers. Drake looked on in curiosity. He didn't realise that they had these kinds of feelings.

'How did I?-' She stopped and looked at Scott. 'But you held me and that means, we both don't have any lives left in this game,' she paused and walked on a few paces. 'Where did the life force chip come from to save me?' Scott looked at Crystal and threw his gaze over to Drake.

'Wha-,' she was trying to work it out. Drake realised that they *did* have an almost human side. This was mind-blowing.

'Drake took DROD's life chip, and I put it inside you,' Scott told her.

'I owe you a debt of thanks then, Drake,' Crystal said looking the most vulnerable he'd ever seen her.

'I would have done it for anyone who needed help. That's what we do in my world,' Drake explained thoughtfully.

'Thank you,' she said simply. She turned and smiled at Scott. 'We have to be careful from now on then. No more chances. Right, time to go.' That was it, the extent of the emotion. Crystal had already refocused on the quest. Drake was dumbfounded by their ability to forget something important so quickly, but they were programmed after all. Drake mulled it over in his mind. Crystal and Scott were changing, he knew that. The rest of this journey was going to be interesting if nothing else.

They continued along the sweeping corridor and the light became brighter at the other end. A feeling of relief filled Drake. He hated the thought of darkness all the time. He picked up his pace and kept up with his companions. The brightness of the light hurt his eyes until he got used to it. They stood at the entrance to the next level.

'The rules have changed,' Scott announced.

'What does that mean?' Drake asked.

'It means that we will help you get through the game,' Crystal said. 'We're all in this together now.'

'When did this decision take place? Does this mean instead of fighting me, you're going to help me get out of here?' he looked at both of them curiously.

'It's only fair,' Scott replied. Drake shook his head with disbelief.

'I'll never understand avatars,' he thought to himself.

The tunnel eventually opened out onto a jetty of sorts. It was windy, and Drake finally realised why. There in front of them was a large sailboat, tied to a dock. The deep blue substance it was immersed in though wasn't water. It appeared to look like the sky. They were standing on a jetty high above land and sea. The boat was bobbing up and down in mid-air as if in the ocean.

'Well this is surreal,' Drake gasped and whistled a long tune.

'Yeah, this is new for me too,' Scott added. 'Crazy.'

'Same here,' Crystal chipped in. 'What now? Do we get inside?'

'I guess we get on-board. I don't see any alternative,' Drake concluded.

'Yeah there's nowhere else to go, by the look of things,'

Scott said whilst looking around at the new backdrop.

'Where are we now?' Crystal mumbled.

'Maybe we should go back,' Drake reasoned. Then he remembered his watch. In all the confusion he'd forgotten he was on a time limit, and so had the others by the look of things. He looked at the flashing amber dot on the mapping reference. It was still ahead of them, but closer than it had ever been. The time was slowly running out, he had thirty minutes left before, well he didn't know what.

'It's not backwards we have to go. Looking at my GPS, our destination is straight ahead. And there's only half an hour left and counting. We've got to get a move on, guys.'

Scott and Crystal looked at their watches too.

'It's moving off,' Crystal added.

'Yeah it's getting away all right,' Scott said nodding.

'Boy, this place is weird. Things come and go at will,' Drake uttered, looking daunted. 'Well, there's no option, is there really? It's the boat, and that's it.'

Scott steadied the craft while Crystal and Drake clambered on-board. Drake tried not to look down. Everything in this world seemed to do with heights. He didn't have Vertigo, but climbing aboard a sailboat in the middle of the sky was scary stuff. One slip and that would be the end unless the wings opened up again, and he wasn't prepared to take that chance. They helped Scott on after he'd untied the rope. They had to be quick because as soon as the tether was loose; the boat began to drift with the breeze, away from the jetty. Scott slumped into the boat with a thunk! Crystal and Drake fell into fits of laughter.

'Laugh it up, why don't you?' Scott said as he righted himself, looking red-faced from his experience.

'Come on Scott, you would have laughed if it was any of us,' Crystal commented.

'Yeah well,' was all he had to say to that. They were right. Of course, he would have.

The boat was drifting as if pulled by a current, which it was in a way, in an ocean of air. It tilted and bobbed along the same as a normal sea vessel.

'How do we guide this thing?' Drake asked. He was peering over the edge at the far view of the land below. He popped his head back in and then noticed the handle at the rear of the craft. 'It's got a rudder, like any normal boat,' he said knowingly. It had a long wooden handle, which he'd remembered seeing once on a boat in a lake. That one was powered by the wind too, but in the normal way a boat should be. Drake remembered that the sailor eased the rudder with gentle and precise movements. He recalled it particularly well because the man looked so in control and relaxed. Drake's own life was filled with moving here and there and he wanted to feel that content. He came back to reality when Scott chirped up.

'Yeah, but I mean we're in mid-air. That would work in water, how's it supposed to work in the sky?' Scott enquired sensibly.

'One thing I've learned about this mad world is that anything can work here,' Drake admitted.

'There's only one way to find out, let's try it out.' Crystal grabbed the handle and yanked it to the left. The boat started veering and tilting at the sudden movement.

'Wow take it easy Crystal,' Drake told her, 'slow and gentle,' he said as he guided her hand with his. She looked at him and gave a warm smile. Drake realised what he was doing and snatched his hand away as if he'd been burned by something hot. He felt embarrassed and a tinge of red encompassed his cheeks. Scott grinned at him and Drake looked away for a moment, a grin filling his face too.

Soon the weather changed from the lovely, blue and tranquil summer sky to a dirty, charcoal grey. Daylight was soon swallowed by swirling, darkened clouds and cloaked the twilight.

'What's happening guys?' Crystal asked cautiously, looking at the changing skyline. The sail was transformed from a flat sheet into a belly of air and began flapping wildly.

'I don't like this,' Drake commented.

'Me neither,' Scott agreed. A rapid easterly wind came out of nowhere and began pummelling the little boat as if a child was playing with a toy.

'Hold on, everyone,' Drake shouted through the whistling of the whipping breeze. 'Let me take the rudder.' He quickly sat down and took control. Crystal moved over and held onto the side for support. To make things worse, a heavy downpour of rain suddenly added to the deadly cocktail. This was a grave situation and all three of them felt fear.

The boat was flicked and dipped into the swell.

Lightning and thunder flashed on a canvas of grey, adding to their misery.

'Where did this crazy weather come from?' Drake's voice could just about be heard above the bombardment. He held on as tight as he could. Scott grabbed hold of Crystal.

'Get on the floor Crystal and hold on to the sides.' She didn't argue and for once did as she was asked. Scott sat alongside Drake and gripped the rudder to keep it as steady as they could.

'I hope we can keep control of this thing,' Drake half-shouted into Scott's ear. The vessel was being thrown around violently and they were finding it difficult to keep it steady. Drake's face glistened as the water slapped at his cheeks. He rubbed his eyes to focus. His normally wild, black locks were flattened and plastered to his head. Scott looked at him, his eyes blinking with the flecks of raindrops. He was struggling to keep the boat straight, even with the strength of the two of them.

'It's going to tip over, isn't it?' Crystal screamed at them in the deluge.

'Just hold on, it'll soon blow over,' Drake assured her. Even with her rain-soaked face and the drops dripping off her nose, she still looked beautiful, which slightly distracted him from the danger. The boat tilted violently to one side, and all three were caught unaware. Crystal fell completely over the side. Scott looked on helplessly but was relieved to see her fingers grip the edge of the boat.

'Crystal don't let go,' Scott called out. The boat stayed

vertical and he could kneel and still hold on. She looked at him with her eyes wide. He quickly grabbed her wrist and pulled her up slowly. Drake could do nothing to help; he was holding on with both hands to the other side of the boat. He was afraid that if he let go, he would fall out.

'Are you two alright?' he screeched.

'I've got you,' Scott grunted as he wrestled Crystal back into the craft. The boat itself was more or less at a ninety-degree angle. The rain was lashing hard and fast and felt like hail against their skin. One second they could see in the brilliance of a lightning flash and the next, they were pitched into complete darkness again.

'Everyone lean to one side,' Drake cried out. With that, all three of them heaved their weight in one direction. 'Come on, push,' he shouted. To their surprise and joy, the boat levelled back off and they were the right way up again. But it wasn't long before a huge swirl of wind surged in and flicked the sailboat into a tailspin.

'Hold on,' Scott bellowed.

'I'm trying,' Crystal retorted, 'but all this spinning is making me feel giddy.' Drake was holding on to the mast and trying not to throw up in the process. The little craft spun round and round-faster and faster.

'I can't keep hold of the boat much longer,' Drake screamed.

'It's going too fast,' Crystal squeaked. Both Scott and Drake tried to hold the sides of the boat with one hand and grip Crystal with their other hands. But it was an impossible task. It was spinning at such a speed that all three of them were eventually catapulted out into the angry sky. They were separated, and the sheer suction of the current pulled at them. Soon they were swallowed by the wind and fell to earth. Down they went and splash landed into the sea. To their horror, the wind had whipped up a whirlpool. None of them was in any state to think and had to go with the flow. Their tired bodies were sucked under the water in the same motion as emptying a plughole in a washbasin. It was black, cold, and they couldn't hear or feel anything. Where on earth were they?

Drake came to and felt the sensation of being pulled through something. He could feel his senses returning. As the water level dropped, he found that he was swimming along a long cylinder. He coughed, spat water and hungrily sucked in the fresh air that seeped in. I must be alive; he was so disorientated he didn't know whether he was or not. Where are the others? He thought. He found, as things began to calm, that he was on his own. The water tube was only half-full. Drake found that he could breathe a lot easier and could swim along with the flow. Where was the pipe leading? He naturally swam breaststroke. He kept going but didn't know how long he had to keep it up for. It was getting lighter further down. Where would this lead?

Chapter 10: Solo

Full daylight filtered into the tunnel as Drake drifted along. He finally came to a dead end in the pipe and began treading water. Drake gasped and gulped for air-his voice echoed along the hollow tube. He could hear the water in the background, gushing and draining away into another pipe, he assumed. He flipped over and dove down to the base of the pipe, following the pull of the water. It took him back a couple of metres. He searched the base only to find a small grid where the water filtered through. He knew that he couldn't get out that way; it was too small to fit through. He swam back to the surface, the cold air chilling his cheeks. He looked up and saw that above him was a cut-out in the pipe. Through half-closed eyes, he could only make out a pure white bar of light, no shapes or shaded areas. Drake's heart sank. He could see his predicament. The circumference of the tunnel was too great, so he couldn't stand on the bottom. He had to somehow reach up, grab the cut-out and pull himself up. There were no grips to speak of or any way of climbing up the smooth, curved inner wall. He realised that once his strength was gone, he would eventually sink and drown.

'HELP! Please help me. Scott, Crystal, can you hear me?' he called out in-between gulps of water. 'Please, I'm stuck in here.' There was no answer, and he felt so alone. 'I'm going to die here,' he said, his sickly voice echoing along the endless length of the tube. Once he stopped complaining, all he could hear was the lapping and dripping of water.

'Aaaaaaargh,' he screamed in frustration and sank under the water again, eventually hitting the bottom. Drake pushed himself back up, and when he floated on the surface, he began to calm down. His foot hurt. This isn't helping, he reasoned. Then something occurred to him. In the middle of his rant, deep underwater, he felt something against his right foot. What was it? Ignoring his pain, Drake dog paddled past the slot of light which gave a clear view. The water was perfectly translucent. He didn't know how that could be possible; he'd just come from the sea. But he wasn't going to question anything anymore. This world wasn't normal, not like the real world, his world. He gazed into the water, and when the ripples settled, he saw some kind of wheel. It was on a shaft, raised above the inner surface, that's why he caught his heel against it.

'What does that do?' he felt himself asking. Drake didn't wait any longer and took a deep breath. He dived down and grasped the small wheel. He tried to turn it to the right, but it wouldn't budge. Then he tried left, but his breath was running out. He was sure that he felt a slight movement. He swam straight to the surface again. His breathing was rapid, and his mind filled with wonder.

'It moved, I'm sure it did,' he said spitting water from his dripping mouth. He closed his eyes and rubbed away the excess and also wiped the snot from his nose. With no time to waste, Drake sucked a long, deep lungful of air and dived below once again. He grabbed the metal circle tightly and gave a huge twist to the left. It loosened, and he twisted it as fast as he could. His lungs began to burn again, but there was movement in the water and bubbles were gurgling to the surface. Drake couldn't stay down there any longer and fought his way back up. He broke through the surface again, water cascading from his body. He looked around and saw the level on the side was falling, but slowly. Drake dipped down to the valve and twisted until it stopped. There was a swirl of movement, like an open plughole. He didn't have to swim far this time, and he soon found he was touching the bottom. It was strange feeling the water pull at his body as it subsided. He was drained of strength and shaking with cold. Eventually, he was left standing in an empty, metal tunnel. The excess water dripped from his wet suit, leaving a small puddle at his feet. Drake looked around and then up again. That was the only way out. The end wall was only just ahead of the escape route, so he knew what he had to do. He took a few steps back until he was far enough to run. He sprinted towards the wall and dived at it with his left foot. As soon as he hit the surface, Drake kicked off and pushed himself up towards the opening. To his surprise, he reached out and grabbed the edge first time with both hands. He held on tight and wasn't going to let go for anyone. Not thinking about it, he pulled himself up into the light and climbed up in one go!

He was out! Drake gasped for air and lay in one spot on the ground for a while, to get his breath and strength back. When he was ready, he stood up, but his body was still tired and aching. Drake looked around. Where was he? And where were the others?

'Hello, anyone. It's me, Drake,' he cupped his hands as he shouted to amplify his voice.

This place was only partly lit. It felt like being underground, but it wasn't a rock-like formation; it was more like solid concrete. He'd seen places in movies like this, secret government facilities. The ground was flat and even, but there were at least five different ways he could go. Circular openings surrounded him, but he couldn't see beyond ten metres in any direction. Drake wiped his hair away from his eyes and urgently checked the GPS on his wristwatch. The dot was close, and this gave him hope.

'I'm gaining, it's not that far away,' he said. He looked at the clock, and his heart sank. He had twenty-three minutes left. It was hard to believe that from getting on the boat to where he was now had only taken seven minutes. Time seems to move slower than expected in this game, he reasoned. But that was of no consequence now, and neither was attempting to find the others. He couldn't think about Crystal and Scott, he needed to finish the game and get back home; after all, they would live again for another game. He looked at his suit and realised it was almost dry. He looked at his watch again. The GPS revealed a network of roads with the amber dot hovering at a crossover point.

It's suddenly stopped! Drake looked on curiously. 'Why has that happened?' he wondered. 'Is this my chance to catch it, whatever *it* is?' He walked from one opening to the next, holding his watch to each entrance. Which one was the one to take? He continued, nothing-nothing. When he got to the fourth opening, the watch bleeped like a dog finding a bone.

'OK then, this is it,' he spoke with confidence, getting into the habit of talking to himself. He set off and ran at a steady pace, his light rubber boots slapped against the ground, letting out a series of echoed squelches. He jogged along the ground but kept checking his coordinates. He followed the dot as if his life depended on it, which it probably did. Everywhere looked the same and an empty feeling consumed the pit of his stomach. The lighted passageways tapered off in many directions, but he kept to the true path, or so he thought.

He was putting a lot of faith in a flashing dot on a white background. He had nothing else to help him since he'd lost Scott and Crystal and that still hurt. Drake bounced along at a steady pace. He couldn't hear anything except his own echoed footsteps and heavy breathing. He was gaining though, and that made him smile and filled him with encouragement to continue. There was a sweeping bend just ahead and Drake's excitement heightened when he looked down. The dot was only a matter of twenty or so metres away. But when he raised his head to see what was coming up… CLANG! Everything went black.

He opened his eyes and tried to focus; he was woozy. He swallowed hard and blinked. His head hurt. He gingerly touched his forehead and immediately winced. There was a lump emerging, and it was wet and sticky. He looked at his hand and saw streaks of blood glistening on his fingers.

He also felt sick and instantly threw up. Drake wiped his mouth after he'd finished and leaned back against the tunnel wall. His chest was heaving from running. He touched his head again; the lump was still there. 'Why wouldn't it be?' he said in a dry croak. 'That's going to give me a headache when it's stopped burning,' he grumbled. He didn't feel good, but he knew he couldn't stop now. He still had to find something, the dot; he had to find the dot. It was all coming back to him.

He tried to lift his arm, which felt like it weighed a ton. When he could fully focus, he looked at the watch face. There were eighteen minutes left, and the dot was slowly moving away again. He had to get back on his feet. He got up, still a little woozy, but that would soon subside. His head throbbed like thunder and the broken skin felt partly numb and also burned. Now he could see what he'd hit. It was a metal grid that stood between him and his way out! That was bad enough, but then he heard a low groan somewhere. He thought it was his imagination at first, but then he heard it again. Drake kept still and strained his ears. There was someone in there.

'Who's there?' he called into the darkness. There was shuffling and groping inside the black.

'Drake, is that you?' Crystal called out. He couldn't believe it.

'Crystal, are you OK? Is Scott in there with you?' he shouted urgently.

'I-I think I'm fine. No, Scott isn't in here, he's not with you?' she sounded confused.

'No, I lost the two of you when I fell out of the boat. Where are you? I can't see you,' Drake was getting agitated. He felt helpless again. After all, if she was on the other side of the grid which he presumed she was; how was he going to get to her?

'I'm in here,' she squealed.

'How do I get to you?' he cried. Suddenly his watch began flashing and he couldn't understand why. So, he tapped the lens, just in case it was broken. To his amazement, the face raised itself, revealing a button and a small nozzle.

'What on earth?' Drake looked on in amazement. The button had the word laser pulsing away in red and on the strap in yellow… eye movement! Drake was so confused he pressed the button, anyway. The minuscule barrel followed his eye line and fired a low white light into the sidewall and Drake let go of the button, instantly. A small chunk of masonry fell to the ground, and Drake was gobsmacked!

'Good grief.'

'What's happening?' Crystal shouted out. 'Are you all right?'

'Yeah, I'm fine. Get back as far as you can from the bars,' he warned. He lifted his arm and focused on the first bar of the grid. The excitement built up inside as he pressed the button again. There was another shaft of light which burst from the watch. The yellow glow from the cannon lit up the tunnel. Drake then realised that the visor had dropped over his eyes, protecting his cornea with a filter. The same filter that welders wear when working with metal. The laser cut through the metal bar in seconds as if it was plastic.

'Wow, this thing is amazing,' he gushed. The metal's molten remains were still glowing orange, with plumes of greyish blue smoke rising from it. Now all Drake had to do was repeat the sequence on every one. So, he methodically cut through each until finally the last.

'How much longer, Drake?' Crystal called out.

'Won't be long now, I've only got one to do,' he answered. The last bar was the one that held up the entire frame. He realised that when it fell, it would fall on him, so he took a few steps back.

'Crystal, stay where you are. This whole thing is going to fall.'

'OK,' she said. The feathery flame from the watch did its work and the last sliver of steel broke away. The heavy grid came crashing down with an almighty Clang! The wrist laser stopped and returned to its hidden position. Drake didn't waste any time and ran over the fallen metal gate, keeping his head low not to touch the jagged stumps that were still glowing above him.

Crystal was on the ground looking more dazed than he'd just been. He rushed over to help her up. Wow, even covered in dust, bruised and battered she still looked stunning. He tried to shake the thought from his mind.

'You OK?' he asked with concern, reaching out with his hand. 'Nothing broken?'

'Yeah, I'm fine, but I still don't know what happened!' she sobbed. Drake knelt by her side and shook his head.

'Look we'll find Drake and finish this game together,' he lied. What else could he do?

Chapter 11:
Kidnapped

Drake got back on his feet and helped Crystal up. The air was dry with thick dust that tickled the back of his throat-making him cough. He swished away the settling cloud as if swotting an annoying fly. Drake tried to focus on his watch. It was a bit fuzzy at first, partly to do with the dust particles and partially to do with the fact that he'd sustained a head injury. He saw that the dot was on the move. He also noticed that there were only thirteen minutes left on the timer. He ground his teeth in frustration, which only made the tight skin around his wound stretch. And that burned like crazy, which made him want to touch it. He hissed and sucked in air through his teeth. His head throbbed like crazy and he still felt uneasy on his feet.

'We haven't got much time,' he said in a low tone. 'Let's go. There are less than thirteen minutes left. We've got to move now, Crystal,' He wobbled slightly as he spoke.

'You're hurt. How did that happen?' she asked, gawping at the reddened lump on his head. He thought about telling her that he'd run straight into the steel cage, but thought better of it.

'Too embarrassing to mention,' he said sheepishly, but with that, she saw him wince and wobble slightly. Drake closed his eyes but immediately reopened them. He thought that he was going to throw up.

'You're looking awful, come here,' she beckoned for him

to get closer.

'What? I'm fine, Crystal. Look, we haven't time to waste,' he said urgently but had to grab onto her for support.

'You can't function like that. Come here and sit down,' Crystal insisted. There was a concrete ledge which protruded from the wall. It was enough just to sit on.

'Crystal, we haven't time...'

'Shush,' Crystal commanded. Drake didn't have the strength at that point to argue with her and did as he was told. 'Now, close your eyes.'

'Wha...' he was confused.

'Shush I said,' Crystal was more insistent. 'Close your eyes,' she repeated. Drake was hesitant at first but did as he was asked. What was she up to? All manner of things popped through his head. Was she going to kiss him? What would be his reaction? Would he fall over? Would he throw up again? His thoughts were all over the place. His head started spinning and he could feel the bile in his throat begin to rise.

'Oh, I-I,' he tried to get up, but then… everything immediately stopped! All of a sudden, he didn't feel pain, giddiness or sickness or have the feeling of passing out. He felt pretty good!

'All right, you can open your eyes now,' Crystal said softly. Whatever she'd done, it didn't involve touching lips, and he was relieved. He didn't want to be sick when kissing someone. That would've been gross. The thought made him shudder. Her touch didn't involve anything, except a warm tingle. He blinked his eyes open again and looked up at her with suspicion and scepticism.

'You can stand up now,' she said and watched as he got to his feet. He looked at her with penetrating eyes. She peered back and tilted her head slightly to her left shoulder. Crystal squinted and shook her head.

'What?' she asked.

'What did you do? I-I feel different,' he stammered. 'Did you fix me somehow?' he breathed easy and smiled as if a great weight had been lifted. 'This is nuts. I feel great,' he beamed a large smile.

'Feel your head now. It should be better, back to normal in fact.' Drake gently touched the lump above his eye. It wasn't there. It was completely gone. He rubbed the flatness of his forehead.

'Wow. That's amazing,' he said as he dabbed his finger in the general area of the wound, there was nothing to indicate any type of injury.

'How did you do that?' he asked, feeling overwhelmed. 'With no tablets, needles or medicine.' Drake felt his head again, for good measure, but nope, it was completely healed. Well, more than that, it was as if the wound hadn't appeared in the first place. This girl was amazing.

'What are you? Doctor Crystal?'

'We're in a game dummy,' she mocked, 'you can do a lot of things in here,' she pointed to the ground, 'things that you probably can't do out there, in your world.'

'OK smarty pants, pull your neck in,' Drake responded.

'Pull my what?' Crystal was confused. 'Is that another

one of the weird things you say from your world?'

'No, it's not weird. This place is weird. My world is normal.' He shrugged off any thoughts he might have had about kissing her.

'We have to continue to our destination,' she added sounding more like a computer programme again.

'Yeah, I agree. We have to move right now; time is running out.' Crystal checked her wrist and studied the readout. She twisted her body in the direction they needed to go. Drake hadn't noticed before, but the light was different here. He looked up and saw that there was movement from a fan fixed into the ceiling. The continual rotation brought darkness and light in equal measures. But the direction in which they had to proceed looked bleak and dangerous. What else was new? He'd come to expect the unexpected in this world.

'That way,' she said, pointing into the direction he wanted to avoid. Drake took another glance at his timepiece.

'Twelve minutes, that doesn't give us much time,' Crystal said before Drake had a chance to. 'We have to keep our wits about us. We don't want any more delays.'

'We can't go without Scott. We have to find him and get him back,' Drake said.

'Forget Scott, we have to finish the game,' Crystal was adamant. 'Wherever he is, you can be sure he'll find us, or he's already been caught,' she said, with no feeling at all.

'What? We can't just leave him,' Drake was appalled at her response.

'Look, Drake, Scott would do exactly the same thing if

it were me or you. The object of the game is to finish before your opponents, and I intend to do just that. Besides, we don't even know where he is,' she said. 'I'm not wasting time looking, he could even be ahead of us–did you think of that?' No, Drake hadn't thought of that. And she could be right.

'But, what if he's not? I've just come to help you, and the two of you told me in the tunnel that we'd all get out together. We should at least have a quick look for him,' Drake rounded angrily.

'That was then, things have changed. I need to go. If you want to look for him, be my guest.' Drake didn't like this side to her one bit. She could be like two different people sometimes.

'I'm going.' Crystal set off in a sprint, checking her wristwatch as she went. Drake knew that there wasn't much time left, so he couldn't really go looking for Scott himself either. He also knew that if he didn't complete the game, then he couldn't go back to his world. It was an awful situation to be in. He didn't like leaving anyone behind, but he had no choice. This game was getting weirder by the second. How did he get himself into this mess? It didn't really matter now, anyway; he was here, and that was that. He made a snap decision and decided to follow in Crystal's wake. He swallowed hard as he entered the tunnel, and the darkness consumed him once more.

Chapter 12:
Tunnel Spiders

Drake chased after Crystal; she was already halfway along the tunnel. She was getting difficult to see in the bleak conditions. His visor once again slid down and gave him a daylight view.

'Hey, wait,' he shouted after her, 'come on Crystal,' but she didn't respond. She was too focused on finding the way out and continuing her mission to capture whatever that dot was hiding. All Drake could do was keep up with her stride.

'I hate tunnels. This game has a fixation with them,' he groaned.

This tunnel was like all the rest of the underground passageways he'd been through already. But as he peered beyond the sprinting form of Crystal's body, Drake could see a minute point of natural light. He stopped to see if there was another way out. The readout on his visor gave him many openings. Dark and scary holes were all around him. This made him shudder. Before he knew what was happening, he heard noises, other than their feet slapping on the ground. The sounds were creepy and unnerving and came from everywhere. The strange constant tapping was like a million tiny feet, all moving at the same time, scuttling along. He didn't like it one bit. His breath came in short bursts and he wiped a layer of sweat from his upper lip.

Drake's visor suddenly switched to x-ray vision, and that was all he needed. To his complete horror, he could see the blueprint of this underground network and that's when it revealed many-many creatures. His breathing became urgent and his eyes felt as though they were trying to pop out. He couldn't see exactly what they were until he zoomed in. And what he feared most in the world revealed itself, spiders! But these were unlike any spider he'd ever encountered before the game. These huge insects had pointed tentacles that could tear and maim with short-hairy legs.

'Oh, good God, I need a weapon,' he said. His wristwatch wasn't giving him any help in that department either. Then he remembered the grid with the steel bars. 'That could work.' He turned and made his way back to where he'd found Crystal, leaving her to continue alone. The metal grid was on the ground where he'd left it. The bars had cooled and weren't glowing anymore. Drake touched one. It was still warm, but he could pick it up. He was just hoping that they were loose enough to pull through the framework. He was in luck. Slowly Drake teased one of the shortest bars and it slid out. He stood up and weighed it in his hand. The bar was about the same length as a baseball bat and weighed twice that. Now he had a weapon. He felt more confident but didn't know if it would make any difference against the sheer numbers.

He quickly got into stride and zoomed after Crystal again. The tapping was getting closer and when Drake looked, he could see she was almost at the end of the tunnel. If he could just catch her, then maybe he could get out of here.

Drake ran through the darkened corridor of the main drag. There were so many holes around him that it reminded him of swiss cheese. He didn't need his visor anymore, and it retracted. He'd never felt so scared in his whole life. His face was a thin layer of sweat, which cooled from the rush of air. He was panting heavily now; not only from running but also because of the fear of being trapped by these creatures.

He ran past the various openings and tried not to look. Amid the darkness, he could see thousands of small disc-like eyes, peering through the dim depths of the channels. The creatures were scuttling along the walls, ceiling and ground of each section. Their small, stubby legs could move at a fair pace. He knew it was him they were targeting. He wasn't going to make it! They were pouring out of the tunnels beyond and behind. He realised that he was surrounded. He felt like he was going to cry.

'This is it. I'm going to die a horrible death,' he said shakily. Drake's panicking overwhelmed him. What should he do? What should he do? His attention was caught by another flashing light on his wristband. The watch had turned itself into laser mode again.

'Oh my God,' he exclaimed. 'It's about time.' A soothingly, warm feeling of hope consumed him. But there were so many. How was he supposed to defend himself when he was the only one? He tossed the bar to the ground, and it made an echoed clang as it impacted. He knew that he couldn't use the laser and the club at the same time. He readied himself for battle as his enemy closed in.

Crystal was about to exit the tunnel and continue with the game. But something made her turn around just before she broke out. It was difficult to see much detail from within, with the glare of the outside. But she could make out little disc-like stars that twisted and moved. Her software quickly informed her that the luminous stars were a mass of glowing eyes. She had all she needed to know; Tunnel Spiders. She was in a dilemma! Should she exit and leave Drake to cope on his own? Or should she go back and help him? This went against the rules of the game, but this game was like no other she'd ever been involved in. For a moment she froze, her programming in turmoil. It was like her systems were working against each other. She finally made her decision.

Drake stood his ground. There was no way now he could get past the hordes of insects. He could hear them and feel them crawling from all directions. He spun around and let off a few blasts, which lit up the tunnel like a firework, revealing his worst fears. Three or four of the creatures peeled from the walls and crumpled onto the ground. But that strike was just a drop in the ocean. There were thousands more of the miniature electronic insects appearing from all angles. There was wave upon wave of them.

He fired random shots, and the bugs were falling, but not fast enough. He had to fire and move forward, at the same time cutting a channel towards the exit. One landed on his shoulder and he immediately punched it off. They were overhead and he could see their horrible insect faces, only metres away. He concentrated on a series of blasts which ripped a line through. When the laser light hit the creatures, they sparked and the luminous eyes dimmed, rendering them dormant. Drake was holding them back to a point, but more were moving in and no matter how hard he tried, he couldn't keep them at bay.

'Jesus, get away from me,' he screamed as he let off another volley of lightning strikes. Up close, he could hear them; clicking and buzzing, their demon eyes penetrating. It was horrible. Drake swept along the tunnel with another bank of laser-fire. The spiders were slowing a little, but not enough to help him escape. Just as he thought things were improving, more came. He was being swallowed up, and it seemed impossible to retaliate. His head was full of their gnawing sounds, grinding into his thoughts. In all the frenzy, he felt a sharp pain in his calf. It took his attention away from the fight, and to his horror, he could see one locked onto his leg. The pain was excruciating, and Drake screamed out in agony.

'Get off me you stinking beast,' he yelled and pointed the laser directly at it. It sparked and fell away, crumbling to dust. One-two-three more climbed onto him. On his back, right leg and arm. He frantically fought them and smashed against the side of the tunnel wall. He managed to get two of them off. He fell backwards and crushed the one attached to his shoulder blade. He heard the crunch of a shell and the screech rung in his ears. The satisfaction didn't last, it was hopeless, and they were quickly on him. Drake had one more last ditched attempt at fighting off their tearing, biting molars. He felt like a piece of meat tossed into a cage of hungry dogs.

He'd all but fought his last blow, screaming in defeat, the pain overwhelming. His laser dimmed, but there were beams of white light overhead. Suddenly, he could see a shift in the movement of the spiders. They stopped attacking and began backing away. They weren't biting anymore, and that was a relief in itself. He found it difficult to react and was drained of energy. The flashes of colour were more intense, and Drake could see the urgent shuffle of retreat. He came back to his senses for a moment and started firing bursts of his own again. They were moving back into the tunnel, and gaps appeared. He felt strange, as if his limbs weren't part of his body.

'Drake-Drake, are you alright?' Crystal called out. Was he dreaming? This boosted him into action, and he climbed to his feet. The blasts of light gave him some perspective of where he was in the tunnel. But the ground seemed to move underfoot, and he couldn't work it out. His head was swimming, his ears buzzing and when it became too much, his body collapsed to the ground in amongst the dead carcasses. He couldn't move a muscle. Everything around darkened to black, and he felt himself drifting off. He could hear someone calling him from far away.

'Drake, wake up.' It was getting further away, and sleep felt like a luxury to his aching limbs. It was warm here and comfortable. Why should he wake up? Beep-beep-beep-beep. What was that annoying sound? Someone was calling him, and now there was an alarm to wake him up. Why don't they leave him alone, just for another five more minutes? Beep-beep-beep-beep-beep-beep-

'Stop-stop,' he felt himself saying. But it kept on annoying him.

BEEP-BEEP-BEEP-BEEP-BEEP-BEEP-BEEP-BEEP! It was so loud that it was hurting his ears.

'Stop it–stop it,' he said and opened his eyes. Everything was a greyish blur. There was someone or something blocking his vision, but he couldn't make it out at first.

'DRAKE, wake up, wake up.' Who was that? It sounded like–it was Crystal!

'What's happening? Are you OK?' he asked her.

'Am I OK?' she smiled and as Drake focused, her white teeth and perfect cheekbones came into view. He went to get up but found he couldn't move anything, only his mouth seemed to work.

'I can't move,' he bleated.

'You've been zapped by tunnel spiders Drake, no wonder you can't move. If it were me or Scott, we would've been destroyed,' she informed him.

'What does that mean? Am I going to stay like this and die here?' he said, feeling scared.

'No. I can counteract it with a boost from my system. That should bring you to full capacity again. It's whether I should or not is the question,' she deliberated.

'What do you mean?' he asked.

'Well, I'm guaranteed to win this game with you and Scott out of the way.' Drake closed his eyes and sighed.

'Go then and leave me here.'

Her eyes glowed for only a split-second, which looked cool from Drake's perspective. It made her even more attractive. Then her cold expression changed from a frown to a relaxed grin.

'What's happened?' he asked curiously.

'Nothing now get up,' she insisted.

'I-I can't,' he reacted.

'Yes, you can, Drake. Now we haven't got much time left, so GET UP,' she was most insistent. Drake found he could now actually move his body. It was a great relief. Also, his head didn't hurt anymore or feel dizzy. She'd done it again.

Without even thinking about his actions, Drake flung his arms around her and gave the biggest hug he'd ever given anyone. Crystal was taken completely by surprise and instinctively pushed him away.

'Wow, take it easy,' she squeaked.

'I thought that was it. I was paralysed, and for a moment I thought that I would never walk or do anything again. It frightened me, Crystal. I also thought you were going to leave me in here with those-those…' he couldn't say anymore. Tears welled up in his eyes.

'OK, I understand, you were frightened. But you're fine now. You've just got to man up and deal with it, for crying out loud,' Crystal replied coldly. Drake wiped his eyes and tried to compose himself.

'OK, that was a moment that I'd like to forget about if that's alright with you?' he felt embarrassed.

'It's fine with me,' Crystal replied shaking her head. Drake knew that she was only initially a computer programme, but he'd found that there was some human emotion creeping into her psyche, if that were possible.

'All right then, we have to go,' he reasserted. They had a job to do, and there wasn't much time left to do it.

Chapter 13: Spinning disk

They stood in a quiet tunnel now. The last of the scuttling insects were gone, and all that was left were the corpses of the fallen. Luckily for Drake, his suit protected him from the vicious attack of the insects, and his only injuries were bruises. He was so tired, and his whole body ached. Even though Crystal had healed him, some things had to heal on their own. After all, he wasn't a programme. Being human gave different values. Crystal's body was a different thing altogether. She would rejuvenate as the game progressed.

The two companions crunched over the carcasses of their enemy and finally made it to the end without any more incidents. As they approached the bleaching white light of the outside, Drake looked at the timer. His heart flipped, and a real sense of dread washed over him. He swallowed hard as reality set in.

'We've only got seven minutes left, Crystal,' He couldn't conceal the sound of fear in his voice. 'The dot is moving away, look.' Crystal checked hers to confirm it.

'We may as well forget it. We'll never make it now,' he looked despondent, the lines on his forehead told the story.

'Nonsense. Let's carry on and see what we're up against. There's still time,' she said. Real determination was in her tone. Drake loved her tenacity, but in his heart of hearts, he didn't believe they could make it.

This section of the game opened up into a whole new world, and the light was blinding. Drake shielded his eyes and squinted.

'Ow, that is so much more painful than the insects,' he winced. Crystal didn't have to squint; her retinas automatically adjusted. When he finally grew accustomed, he was taken over by what he saw. It wasn't as he'd expected at all. Everything in here seemed gigantic. He looked at Crystal, and she gazed back with the same sense of the unknown. They were standing on a ledge of sorts, only a metre or so from the tunnel entrance. The first strange thing was that the ground was moving, just beyond the rim. Crystal was scanning the area, studying the surrounding floor and above. Drake, on the other hand, found it very disorientating. He had to seek support from the wall, trying not to fall over. He couldn't look down for too long because it made him feel dizzy. He'd already thrown up twice so far and didn't want to again.

'Aww,' he groaned, his head swimming.

'You all right?' Crystal asked, looking at him with concern. 'You look a bit green, that's not your normal colour,' she probed.

'Yeah, I'm fine, green is good. It's just a little bit overwhelming,' he said, trying his hardest to keep his eyes level with Crystal's. 'What is this thing, anyway?' Drake took a renewed interest whilst trying not to focus too much on the spinning ground below. He craned his neck and looked at his surroundings. The ground, as he called it, wasn't ground at all. It was a giant spinning disk that revolved at speed, like a huge roulette wheel. Place your bets-place your bets. The words shot through his mind for some reason. He continued searching, trying to find an escape route. The walls were high and smooth, so Drake did an intensive scan. He couldn't find any place for climbing out of here. God, it's hopeless, he thought.

'We're never going to cross this way. We'll have to go back,' he said. 'There's just no way through,' But the moment he uttered the words, the entrance to the tunnel shut with a clang! A steel barrier had slid out from the left side and sealed shut! Drake turned and slammed his hands against the panel. It was no good-it was solid.

'Oh, bloody great,' he cursed, screwing up his face with annoyance. 'There's no going back that way either, by the look of things.' Drake stood silent. Normally he would have had a backup plan of some sort, but the more he ran things over in his head, the more it felt hopeless. Seven minutes wasn't much time, and it was trickling away like sand in a sieve.

'Come on, we can fly out of here, easy,' Crystal smiled confidently. For once Drake was jealous. Why hadn't he thought of that? He was also sceptical of what would happen if things went wrong. And with that, Crystal lurched forward into what she thought would be a full take-off. But, to her complete surprise, she only dropped forward. Luckily Drake noticed and grabbed her before she fell flat on her face. He clamped his arms around her and pulled her in. They fell against the metal door of the tunnel.

'Uh, what's happening? Why can't I fly? Why can't I fly?' she repeated and gave Drake a bewildered look. He just shrugged his shoulders. This was worse. They couldn't fly out and the only way forward was across the spinning floor.

'There must be different rules for each level. But even though we've been stuck in various places, we've always managed to get through. There has got to be a way out of here somehow,' Drake said as he tapped his top lip in thought.

He looked around again and saw that directly across from them was an opening at the centre of this vast room. He squinted and his visor typically slid down; he loved that about this world. He could now plainly see what predicament they were in. He arched his right brow, smiled and nodded in appreciation as a plan was formulating in his head. The opening led through to another entrance that would take them from this section to the next. He zoomed in and saw that to the right of the second entrance was a button. It was a red flashing light with words stamped in bold letters on the plastic: Time Freeze Fifteen Minutes. This was overlaid in white text. Crystal had noticed it too.

'Does that mean that if we hit the button, then we get an extra fifteen minutes to complete the game?' Drake enquired, as he was not familiar with these levels.

'Looks like it,' Crystal replied, not sounding too confident. Drake checked his watch again. There were only five minutes left of the countdown. His stomach twisted every time he looked.

'We've got to get across this Crystal. Are you ready for this?' Drake was poised on the edge, as an athlete set for a sprint.

'I was born ready,' Crystal answered. Drake looked at her sceptically.

'Really, born ready? Nobody uses that expression anymore.'

He was still shaking his head as they pushed off in unison. He needed the best spring action to propel his body as far as he could. Crystal being engineered, unlike him, would probably get much further. With one great big push, they leapt almost halfway along the distance. Drake felt chuffed that Crystal didn't get any more spring that he did and dropped down on the same spot.

But the landing they were preparing themselves for didn't happen! Instead of hitting the smooth surface of the spinning deck, as expected, they fell *straight through* it! It was a total illusion. There wasn't even time to scream as things were happening so fast. Down and down the two descended. Drake covered his eyes a split second before he hit the bottom and felt the thud of impact. He lay there motionless. He wanted to open his eyes but was finding it hard to breathe. The crash landing had knocked all the wind out of his lungs. Panic set in just as he found his breath. Why wasn't he dead? Should he open his eyes? He heard Crystal's smooth melodic voice beside him.

'What is this place?' she shrieked. Drake looked but

couldn't answer for a moment.

'Jes-us,' he panted, 'wh-at,' he sucked in as much oxygen as he could, 'what happened?' he gasped, 'that floor-wasn't even real.'

'I didn't expect that.' Crystal sat next to him, looking puzzled.

'Well, me neither. It kind of fooled me too,' Drake said when he got his breath back. Crystal flicked a finger at her monitor. The white screen lit up her face and reflected her creamy-white complexion. Time was almost up! The watch was counting down the last few seconds.

'Game over,' she groaned.

'But it can't be Crystal. We're still here aren't we?' Drake said examining his body.

'Hold on,' she was gazing at the screen. 'now my screen is showing four noughts,' she said as the last second melted away. 'You're right, we are still here,' she looked confused again. 'This has never happened before. I should have faded away, ready to play another game.'

'If you are still alive, then there must be a chance for both of us to finish. We have to get back up there and punch that button. Or...' Drake stopped and realised.

'Or what?' she asked, biting her lip.

'Or we'll be stuck here forever, that's what,' he said.

'How are we going to get up there without flying, genius?' Crystal snapped. 'I can't fly, and you are just as useless.' Drake looked at her with hurtful eyes.

'Oh, gee thanks Crystal, you are such a comfort,' he jeered back. 'You are part of the computer programme, so you should know what to do. What do you suggest?' he growled flippantly.

'I-I don't know,' She looked defeated and vulnerable, tearful even, for the first time since he'd come into contact with her. He felt awkward. 'I guess I'm supposed to know, but I don't.'

'Look Crystal, I haven't got all the answers either.' He looked up to the top of the hole. They were in a pit of sorts; it was at least thirty feet high with smooth walls and no possibility of any grip. There's no way of climbing out of here, he thought.

'I can't stay here forever. I have to get out. I have to finish the game,' she screamed with desperation.

'So do I don't forget. I don't want to be stuck in this game forever either. I have a life outside of this world that I want to get back to.' Drake was serious. When he thought about it, he missed his mum and his grandparents. And... the school, if he was honest with himself.

'Well, do something about it then?' Crystal exploded angrily and pushed him in the chest with frustration. He wasn't expecting her response and went flying backwards, almost cracking his back against the wall. He only just managed to get his hands behind him in time to soften the blow. He looked back at her with distaste.

'What did you do that for? Are you crazy?' he spat angrily.

'S-sorry, I don't understand what's got into me,' she sobbed and looked more stunned than he did. He was just about to push off the wall and straighten up. Then he noticed that he couldn't move. He twisted his head to look over his shoulder to see what the problem was, but his fingers were embedded into the surface of the wall!

'What the heck is this now?' He pulled and pulled, which took some effort. When he did finally pull his hands from the suckered holes, he examined the finger dents. It appeared that he'd pushed into a foamy surface. But the suction was like an adhesive. This gave him an idea.

'What are you doing?' Crystal asked trying to look over his shoulder.

'It's this wall, it's got a really weird surface,' he answered. 'Kind of sticky.'

'So what?' Crystal was in no mood for riddles.

'If I'm right, we can climb out of here,' he said with a grin looking back at her.

'What do you mean? How?' she was intrigued.

'I'm not sure, but if the wall was strong enough to hold me against it, then maybe it can take our body weight. I don't know, but there's only one way to find out,' he said. She walked beside him and sized up the wall. They could see the button flashing away in the distance. It was the dangling carrot they had to touch to get out of there.

'Are you ready?' he asked. 'And please, don't say born ready.' She grinned. Drake went first and touched his hand to the surface. Would this finally get them to where they needed to go?

Chapter 14:
The climb

Drake looked up and swallowed, but his mouth was dry. It was a long way to the top. He shook the thought from his mind and focused. He reached up, extending his arm and applied pressure with the four fingers of his right hand. He pushed into its foam-like surface, looking for a grip. It took quite a bit of pressure to get as far as the second knuckle. He pulled his body weight, and it held.

'That's how far my fingers have to go to take my weight,' he whispered to himself. Crystal looked on with interest. He turned to face at her.

'It seems to be strong enough to hold me,' he said and kicked the toe of his trainer into the wall, around knee height. The pressure of his foot dug in much easier than his fingers. Drake then pushed upwards and forced his outstretched left hand into the wall above his right. He dug his left foot into the foam at waist height. He was now fully sucked into the surface and holding his weight.

'Have a go,' he grunted. Crystal mirrored his movement and soon they were both at the same level.

'What now?' Crystal asked.

'Well, we keep going,' he said with authority. 'Just follow my movements and climb.' He showed her the next section, and she crawled up beside him again. 'Think of it as crawling along the floor, like a baby.' Then he realised that she was never a baby, she hadn't even been born. She was a programme.

'I know what you mean,' she said.

It took some doing, remembering to pull out one hand and make new grip holes with it while doing the same with his foot. Drake felt exhausted after only ascending a few metres, but as soon as he got the rhythm right, it got easier. Ironically, Crystal seemed to have mastered it a lot quicker and was overtaking him.

'Take your time, Crystal,' he puffed. 'You only need one slip and down you go!' She slowed down, and he caught up.

'Let's do this together,' he said after taking a break for a moment. They'd got about halfway when Crystal looked directly across at Drake.

'What's happening?' she asked quizzically. He looked at her curiously, his nose and forehead wrinkled.

'I don't know what you mean,' he answered honestly. 'What is happening?'

'This wall is moving Drake, I'm sure of it,' Crystal looked worried. Drake held station for a moment, keeping his weight on his feet. He hadn't noticed anything thus far; he'd been concentrating on climbing. Suddenly there was a spark of realisation in his eyes. She was right. Things were slowly moving.

'I see what you mean,' he responded. The wall felt as though it was changing its angle.

'I think we'd better go a little faster before it gets any worse.' Drake was scared, but he didn't want his companion to see. If the angle got too obtuse, then he didn't know what would happen to him. Crystal was part of the programme and wouldn't get tired but, she could get injured. He also knew she didn't have any more lives left to lose. If she fell, she wouldn't survive. He was getting tired and his fingers were sore from digging into the wall–a wall that was slowly getting more difficult to climb. He didn't want to, but he had to move at a faster pace. Drake felt the sting of perspiration in his eyes, his hands were clammy, and the tips of his fingers were slowly losing grip. Things were more intense as he picked up speed. The only problem was that the faster they went-the more mistakes they'd make.

They'd made it three quarters of the way up the wall and Drake could see the top much easier. This gave him a lot more confidence. The end was in sight.

'Crystal can you go on ahead?' he took long breaths, 'That way you can pull me up if I'm in trouble,' he said in-between breaths.

'Sure, no problem,' she replied as if she'd done this every day, which she probably did, he thought.

The wall got to such a tilt that Drake could feel gravity pulling at his finger and foot grips. He could also feel the weight of his body being prized away from the wall too. Crystal was at the top and Drake was only a matter of metres away. He didn't know how she was doing it, but she was holding on to something that kept her anchored. How they were going to get out after he got to the top was another problem. For now, though, getting to where Crystal was waiting was the first priority.

'Come on, reach out your hand,' she said, stretching towards him. Drake pulled out his right hand and made a stab for hers. She gripped it, and the hold was solid. By now, the angle was almost horizontal, and Drake was scared to let go of the foothold. He could feel his heart pounding away in his chest; every thud, he thought was loosening his grip.

'Drake, put your left hand here,' she indicated a kind of ladder rung to the left. He reluctantly released his grip and grappled for the bar. He grabbed it and gripped on tight. A huge feeling of relief filled him. 'You have to pull out your feet; come on you can do it,' she squealed in encouragement. He pulled at his legs and both feet released at the same time.

'Aaaargh,' he growled. He was hanging in mid-air. Crystal still gripped his right hand, and he held on with the left to the rung. Please don't let go–please don't let go, he repeated in his head.

Drake's body was weak from all the exercise and punishment he'd received. The pounding he'd already taken would have amounted to a day at the gym. How much more could his body take? He swung in mid-air with all of this going through his mind.

'Drake-Drake, there's a ladder fixed to both sides. All we have to do is climb it,' Crystal was almost screaming. She moved her arm towards the left ladder as far as she could.

'You must grab the bar. NOW!' she bellowed. Drake let go and swung for the ladder but missed. He was hanging precariously by one arm; inside his head he was screaming. He knew how far the fall was below, and that spurred him on not to let go.

'Drake grab it-grab it!' Crystal was hysterical. His left arm was way too tired, and he didn't know if he could. He made one last attempt and lurched forward. This time he managed to grasp it. It felt exactly like the monkey bars in a park he'd visited once. Using all of his concentration, he willed his right hand to move up a rung, then his left, and so on. The burning sensation in his muscles was overwhelming. You can do it, Drake told himself. Now he could grip with his foot too and eventually could feel both feet on the ladder, easing the strain on his arms. Crystal was already close to the entrance of the next part of the game. Drake grappled his way up so both of them were almost inside.

'Come on, we have to climb through,' she insisted. 'Come on, Drake.'

'Hold on,' he screeched. 'We have to hit the button before we go any further.' She looked at him blankly for a second. A light flickered in her eyes and she remembered.

'Oh yeah, we'll have another fifteen minutes to finish the game.' She was so caught up in the climb that she'd forgotten the most important part.

'Can you reach it from your position?' Drake asked, still struggling behind her.

'I think so,' she responded and extended her arm. She had to stretch to get within touching distance. Drake willed her on. She was so fixated on the task that she let go with her left hand and hit the button at exactly the same time. The wristwatch on Drake's arm flashed up with another fifteen minutes on the screen.

'That's great Crystal, I have the extra time on my-' But she wasn't there anymore. She fell straight passed him. Drake immediately looked on in horror.

'CRYSTAL!' he screamed, but she was disappearing fast. A second or so later and she was gone! Drake stood still, holding the ladder, but alone. A feeling of emptiness consumed him. He cried and bit his lip in anger.

'Crystal,' he called out again, but with a weaker, more sheepish tone this time. There was nothing he could do now; she was just there and now… gone! He couldn't think straight. There wasn't far to go, so he climbed the last few metres and slumped through the doorway into the next level. His mind was awash with all the emotions of someone who'd lost a close friend. What was he going to do now?

Chapter 15:
Stepping stones

Drake heaved himself to his feet and checked his watch. The screen read fourteen minutes and ten seconds. The extra time he'd required was already slipping away, and he grimaced. The dot he'd been chasing for the last hour or so was holding station somewhere just beyond the next level. And the hour itself had felt more like a lifetime with all the obstacles he'd had to contend with. He was so sick of this dot now. Every time he got close, something happened to have his chance snatched away again.

'This game is getting so annoying. It's playing with me,' he grumbled with distaste. Was he ever going to catch this thing? He knew he had to act fast. But losing Crystal was hard and the guilt of not saving her weighed heavy on his heart. He may even have had a bit of a thing for her, silly, but that had slipped away when she fell. He had to forget about everything else and concentrate on escaping from this blasted game. He felt so much contempt for the situation he was in that it gnawed at him. Scott and Crystal were gone; they were both programmes, pixels built up for the purpose of the game. He was human and still alive, and he had to finish it.

'Where am I now?' he said, grimacing, it felt warm here. He looked around and saw he was again on a small plinth. He shuffled his way along the edge, knowing there was bound to be a scary drop attached.

'What the-' the heat hit him fully, and then the fumes. He coughed as the pungent smoke entered his mouth and nose.

'Oh God,' he cried and was about to cover his face when a face mask slid down and protected his exposed features. The top half appeared as goggles and the nose and mouthpiece was a kind of gas mask.

'Wow, this is intense,' he said, but it came out muffled under the headgear. Drake gingerly looked down, but it was difficult to see through the billowing clouds of smoke. At times it thinned, which gave snatches of the landscape. It was a long, long drop, to what he'd expected from the smell of sulphur was lava! He could see the yellows, oranges and smouldering reds of the liquid in a toxic river, calmly flowing along the base. A vast pattern of stepping stones somewhat obscured his vision. They didn't look like the stone slabs from your average garden, that are normally set out in a single row between a pond and flowerbed. No, these were placed in a large pattern, like the hexagonal shapes of a honeycomb in a Beehive.

Their edges weren't touching either; there were half metre gaps between each one. The other odd thing was that they didn't appear to be set on top of the lava. When Drake zoomed in, he could see that the stones floated above the deadly liquid.

'What have I got myself into this time?' he said aloud, his mumblings rebounding from the rock walls of this great canyon. He stared further over and saw there was a way out. This heightened his expectations of maybe finishing the game at last. If the exit was the way out of this nightmare.

The entrance to the next level reminded him of the opening to a church. There were two pillars embedded into the walls on each side, with a beautifully carved stone arch resting above them. In the centre was a crisp, white light, which seemed to beckon him. The depressive colour inside the cave-like structure reflected from the lava below. The orangey, reddish glow gave a sinister and scary impression. In that moment, it wasn't the lava that tormented him but the stepping stones. Before he could get to the exit, he had to negotiate these first. He was really scared, but he was also getting used to that feeling. He'd been scared through this adventure, but he felt so alone now. He stood rigid, not knowing what to do. He weighed things up briefly. The drop was immense. The stepping stones were suspended in mid-air, and time, once again, was against him. He took a long breath before deciding. It was uncomfortably hot in the mask and getting hotter. The lens was steaming up, and the stale odour was making him wretch. He had to get down to the base before he could do anything with the stones. The drop was at least thirty metres and there was no ladder or footholds. It was a sheer cliff edge. Drake thought of the building he'd stood on at the beginning of the game. He, Scott and Crystal had jumped off and floated to the ground. Could he make that happen again? It was one hell of a risk.

'Come on Drake,' he said willing himself on, 'I have to

do this.' Drake shuffled right to the edge. He looked down again and noticed that there was an embankment of about three metres beyond the perimeter of the lava lake. That was where he had to land. Drake took a deep breath-the taste of stale air was horrible. He breathed in short, sharp blasts and ground his teeth together. He slowly leaned forward, his breathing more intense, and he felt himself whimper as he tilted his body. It was too late to pull back now, and he dropped like a stone. His stomach was doing cartwheels. His eyes and mouth were wide open. He tried to scream, but nothing came out. Drake flapped at the wind like a dog paddling across a pond. He could see the lava rushing towards him at a tremendous speed. Drake's mouth was contorted, and his skin stretched tight. All he could do was put his hands pathetically over his goggles to protect himself from the impact, when he suddenly and violently stopped! Drake opened his eyes when he felt his body against something hard. He rolled over and realised that he was on the bank. His breathing slowly returned to normal and he could feel the sweat trickling down his face, inside the mask. He got to his feet; the heat from the lava was intense. The bubbling lake was only a matter of metres away. He would have been blinded if it wasn't for the filter on his visor. There was no time to waste.

He saw the floating stones and tentatively lifted his right foot and extended it out. Now he realised how tired he was; his leg was heavy. It was like lifting a sack of potatoes. When Drake touched the first stone, he lightly grounded his toe on to the surface which wobbled slightly. Drake played with his tongue in his mouth as a distraction, before the leap of faith he was about to undertake. Scenarios flowed through his mind of badly made movies he'd seen in the past. There was always an open lava lake and the possibility of falling into the molten liquid. Every step could mean sudden death, and that made him gulp. The fact that the game was called Death Trap had only just occurred to him. A shiver of nerves raked his body.

On the upside, he'd just jumped the best part of fifty metres and survived. Courage came back in spades and he forgot all his fears-he didn't have time to mess around, anyway. He knew once he'd put all his body weight on there, there was no going back. He had nothing to lose. Drake spread out his arms as if ready to fly, and balance was going to be the key. He nervously breathed in. He put one foot on the stone again and launched his whole body onto the hexagon. The heat from the molten lake made the sweat mist up his goggles, making it hard to focus. Drake had both feet on the small rock which wobbled, but he kept his balance. He settled down and waited for a moment. The hot air from below was making him gag. He hated being too hot. He'd always said that if he had a choice, he would rather freeze to death than boil. Come on, Drake, he urged.

'One down and loads to go by the look of it,' he said with a nervous grin as he scanned into the distance and saw the multitude of floating stones ahead. He reasserted himself.

'OK, on to the next one.' He stepped forward to the

adjacent stone, and it felt as steady as the one he was already standing on. He was a little quicker this time, as he knew time was of the essence. The grin was replaced with a wry smile. The stern expression he'd worn earlier vanished when the confidence returned. The quicker he could navigate this section, the faster he would be out of this sweatbox.

'This is not as bad as I thought,' he said with confidence and continued on to the next in line. That felt the same as the others. He was in a rhythm now and continued to the next; hoping to get this part of the game out of the way. He continued on to the next and the next. Drake looked up and saw that the church entrance was getting tantalisingly close. An excitement warmed his insides, as if the lava wasn't enough. Without thinking, and being way too cocky, he walked straight on to the next stone. It fell instantly under his weight and so did he!

'Aaargh,' he screamed. He didn't know how he'd managed it, but instinctively he'd grasped the edge of the next stone with both hands on the way down. It was holding him and not twisting. The sheer fear of hanging there, only half a metre from death, was heart stopping.

How could he have been so stupid? He thought as he dangled like a loose length of cotton.

'Oh my God, oh my God,' he repeated, but then he started to calm down. He'd realised that all he had to do was to clamber back up. The good thing was that the stone stayed level and hadn't tipped over with his weight. And that meant that it was steady enough. He'd scolded himself enough and beating himself up over this wasn't helping. He also realised that his grip was beginning to weaken.

'Climb up Drake,' he grimaced, straining with every muscle movement. If he could just swing and get his legs to wrap around it, then he could pull himself up, as if he was playing on the Monkey bars in the park. He focused his mind and closed his eyes once again. The problem was that his hands were getting sweatier by the second and the salty perspiration was pooling in his eye sockets; it stung.

He also knew he didn't have much time left. His hands would be so wet in a minute that he'd slip off into oblivion, or his strength would give out. Drake began to swing back and forth, like a clock pendulum.

Drake continued to swing and gain momentum. It was working. He couldn't think about the possibility that his hands could slip at any moment and it would all be over. His feet got closer and closer to the next stone with every swing. One last swing should do it. As Drake got to the peak, he opened his legs and clamped them around the sister stone. He'd made it! The feeling of joy consumed him. He was in an awkward position though. He was still holding on to the previous stepping stone, whilst his legs were clamped to the other. Now the next problem; how was he going to get up on top?

A thought shot through his mind. What if he flipped over? Would that work? Anything is possible, he thought. He could feel gravity pulling his body and his strength fading. He held himself ready and threw all his weight into a roll and with a quick twist; he was back on top splayed across two stones. The feeling of relief was overwhelming!

'I did it,' he gasped in victory. Breathing hard, Drake got to his knees, and in one movement, stood up. He gingerly glanced below and saw the bubbling hot mass waiting for him, but he'd escaped its pull once more. He lifted his gaze and looked straight ahead. He could just make out the weird changing shape of the church arch, through his misted goggles and the heat haze. He wanted to pull off his visor to clear it but knew that if he tried, then the poisonous fumes would kill him there and then-scorching the inside of his lungs. The air inside the mask tasted horrible, and his mouth and throat were dry. He dragged a cough from the back of his throat. What he wouldn't do right now for a cool glass of water. He shook that thought away and concentrated on the job at hand.

He knew he had to go through the same procedure all over again with the rest of the stones, but this time he wouldn't make the same mistake as before. Steadying himself, Drake cautiously moved with precision and stealth. First, he put the right foot forward to test the strength and then the other. It was slow going, and he did become overconfident once or twice, but the fright he'd encountered earlier was still fresh in his mind. The pattern coming to the end had changed, and that brought with it another gut full of nerves.

Drake was left with three stepping stones, but these were three metres apart-one to the middle and one to each side. So that meant all he had to do was jump on one of them; then jump to the end and he was free. But the problem was, which one should he jump on? And would the one he chose be the one to fall? Or would they all fall? He had no idea. This game was cruel. It gave you confidence and then took it away in one swoop.

The mist inside his visor gave hardly any vision. The heat inside his suit was at breaking point. He felt light-headed. He had no choice–he had to pick one. Oh God, this was hard.

'Ingle-angle-silver bangle-ingle-angle out,' Drake said as he pointed from the left side, to the right. He chanted the words he'd heard his mother saying one day when she was working something out in her head.

He stepped back and leapt forward. He forgot everything and just went for it. He landed on the last stone and pushed off without even thinking. The stone held, and he tumbled forward through the air and missed the lava completely. He landed on the hearth of the church. He was out at last and quickly moved on to get away from the heat. Soon everything changed!

Chapter 16: Maze

Drake didn't waste any time; he moved past the pillars and into another different area. The toxic world of the volcano had disappeared, not leaving a trace behind. The claustrophobic confinement of his gas mask had receded, leaving him with a face full of sweat, and a mouth so dry it was difficult to raise spit. What a contrast in this place. There was no unbearable heat or the threat of danger in here. And he was overjoyed at escaping the lava. To his absolute surprise, he stood next to a water cooler. He didn't even think about it and grabbed a plastic beaker and poured out a full cup. He ignored all safety stuff and swallowed. It could have been filled with poison for all he knew, but he was past caring. The water was deliciously cold on the back of his burning throat. That disappeared in no time as he devoured it. He hungrily poured another, and another and gulped it back like swallowing was going out of style. He almost choked at one point and spat out a mouthful. His face reddened, and he breathed hard and fast. He wiped his mouth and chin.

He took time to calm and register where he was now. This was different from the earlier places. He stood at the foot of a white wall, with a gap to his right. He checked his watch and hissed as if he'd burned himself on a hot plate.

'Nine minutes and twenty seconds,' he growled with spittle escaping his mouth. The dot was still hovering–not far on the other side of the wall. It was playing with him.

He shook his head and grunted like some kind of bear. The map on his wristwatch, where the dot waited, looked familiar to him. It was a maze! To Drake's left was a set of steel steps and what appeared to be a balcony. Maybe this could give him a better view, he thought. He dashed and clanked his way to the top and ran along to the middle of the bridge. The whole structure moved underfoot, groaning and screeching with each step. He looked over and rested his hands on the rail. It was indeed set out like a maze. He felt as though he was a king surveying his kingdom. Below was a vast array of corridors shooting off in many different directions. He shook his head in doubt.

'Great,' he said, 'just what I need, a maze. I hate mazes. I never have any bloody luck in mazes,' he cursed and tried to focus on the plan of the labyrinth. He could just about make out the exit; the visor helped. There it was, but where was the dot? Drake was getting sick of this game now; all he wanted to do was go home. He would listen to his mum this time and even try to get along in school. He didn't have any friends there, but he'd try to make some. He hated being alone. He knew it was stupid, but he missed Crystal and Scott, even though they were only avatars. They were the closest he'd had to any kind of relationship and they were gone. He glanced again at his watch; it was just under eight minutes now. He'd wasted enough time and off he shot.

He ran to the stairs, slid his way down the handrail and came to a clunk at the bottom. As expected, it looked different from down here. There was no clue as to where to go. He'd done mazes like these with his mum when dad was away in Germany. He was hopeless, and mum had to rescue him every time. He did have his watch this time and if he hurried, that could help him get through quicker.

'Let's go.' He took the passageway directly ahead and broke into a sprint. What lay ahead? He had to keep his eyes peeled for traps or any kind of danger. This would be his last chance. The game wouldn't give him any more free time, he was sure of it. He ran at a steady pace, keeping his eyes focused. The walls were pure white, like a blank canvas, and split into many corridors. From above he remembered the exit was directly ahead, but from down here it was easy to get lost. Even with glancing at the GPS on his wrist, it was still hard to keep track.

What was that? He heard something and stopped to listen; there was nothing. Was he getting the jitters now too? He'd momentarily got distracted and lost his way. He checked his watch for the umpteenth time and gasped. The screen had gone blank! He stopped in horror. Where was he supposed to go? Drake was in total panic mode when…

'Over here, Drake.' The voice came from ahead, and a clutch of nerves grasped at his abdomen. It was a man! All this chasing and finally he got to hear what he'd been running after. He physically shook and felt so scared that it was hard to breathe.

'Who are you?' He nervously called out, in between panting.

'Come on, over here Drake. You only have to touch me

to get home. That's what you want, isn't it?' There it was again, and it was a man's voice.

'I only have to touch him to get out of here,' Drake whispered. Just touching him would get him home. His head was swimming.

'I'm coming after you,' Drake whispered at first and then he got stronger. He had nothing to lose. 'I'M COMING AFTER YOU!' he shouted with renewed confidence.

'Come after me if you dare,' the voice continued.

'Believe me, I am,' Drake was not at all scared. Drake was way past scared. He was filled with adrenaline.

'I'm waiting,' the voice goaded. Drake ran and followed the voice.

'Here I am boy, come and get me,' it said patronisingly.

'If you're not scared of me, don't keep moving,' Drake bit back. Corridors whooshed past his ears like cars overtaking in heavy traffic. He ran the fastest he'd ever run in his entire life. He came to a sudden stop, almost toppling over in the process!

'Oh, good grief,' he squeaked, 'what now?' He found himself at the entrance of a kind of cul-de-sac. It was circular and held three doors; all identical from their white facade right down to the brass handles. He was so sick of everything. Why couldn't things just be simple?

'Choose one, Drake. One leads out, but the others don't,' the low husky tone was still there.

'Who are you and what do you want with me?' Drake bellowed. 'I've had it with this game. I'll go through a door and still find myself stuck in this bloody game,' he ranted.

'I am the Master.' The melodic dry echo seemed to linger in the air for a few seconds, then dulled to a whisper. 'Come on Drake, you're almost there.'

'Yeah, I've heard that one before. I'm not playing this stupid game anymore,' Drake cried.

'Choose one door Drake, that's all you have to do. The end of the game is near,' The voice of the Master felt so close that Drake thought he was standing next to him.

'Where are you?' Drake questioned again. 'Show yourself.'

'Time is running out for you, Drake,' the Master reiterated. 'Check your watch.'

'My watch isn't working…' Drake looked at his watch and saw it was working again. Six minutes was dissolving into five minutes and fifty-nine seconds. He tried to be clever and opened all three doors. He peered into each one. There was nothing to see inside any of them, except only deep-deep blackness. The watch suddenly seemed to weigh lighter on his arm, as if subconsciously each second was floating away from him.

'Choose a door Drake-time is slipping away!' The master's voice burst through the air like a sledgehammer, and Drake jerked. He felt as if he couldn't breathe. Without thinking, he lurched forward towards the middle doorway and was sucked through. Everything went black and Drake was too scared to even speak. The only comfort was the soft white glow of his watch face. Step by step he eased forward, and only the sound of his irregular breathing was heard. Instinctively he reached out ahead and groped for an exit. A feeling of hope fell like a veil and encompassed his whole body. There was light. Oh, my God. Only a small pinprick, but light all the same. He could feel a smile pulling at each corner of his mouth. He was going to get out, at last. He was going home. Drake's breathing eased and became shallow, the panic he'd felt dissolved. The white dot got bigger and bigger. There was a waft of warm air and the promise of escape. He quickened his pace but didn't run. There could still be danger. By now the light had become a long slit instead of the circle he'd recognised earlier. Was it going to be wide enough to get through? A stab of nerves thumped his stomach again as if it were a physical punch. It had to be the way out, he couldn't go back. The gap *was* wide enough; as he got closer, he could see that. He shielded his eyes from the brightness. He was here, he'd made it. He stepped out of the dark and into the bleached white. It was always bleached white. His eyes hurt and it took a little while to focus. He gradually took his hand away from his face. Where was he now? He got the feeling that it was a big open space, and gusty wind whipped at his face. A nice feeling of joy filled his heart; he must be out of the game. When his eyes began to focus, it was all too much. He dared to look around and couldn't even speak. He stepped out and was standing on a glass-panelled bridge. But below him was... well, he didn't know if he was honest. The small dots in the far distance were moving in a sequence, in lines. And then he realised!

'C-cars,' he stuttered. 'Good grief, little cars.' He was way-way up on a skyscraper. His immediate reaction was to retreat inside the dark, but he couldn't. He could see that the gap he'd just come through wasn't there anymore. Just like all the other levels that this game had pushed him through.

He tried to focus his mind. He'd only just managed to save himself from falling from a great height, on the stepping stones and that was bad enough. This was different. This was in full daylight, on a ledge, hundreds of feet above the ground. He thought back to when he first entered the game; when he jumped off that building and flew to the ground, also in the dark. And he didn't think about what he was doing that time, he just did it. Now there was no choice but to think. He stood there running things over and over in his mind. There was no other way out of this. He was standing on a glass bridge, overlooking a city. The bridge itself wasn't a clear glass as such, but more tinted like the darkened windows in a gangster car from the movies. At the other end was a small ledge that led to an open entrance, and safety hopefully.

Simple really, he thought. Walk across the glass bridge without looking down, he reasoned. And then get out of here. Then two things happened at once. One: Drake could see someone waving to him from the other side. He couldn't make it out at first and when his visor dropped, it was too late. The person had gone! He quickly looked at his watch and saw that the dot he'd been chasing through this game; was the closest it had ever been. It was his target.

Number Two: Well that was fairly obvious. He had to hold out his arms to steady himself. Underneath his feet, the floor was moving, rolling backwards! He found he was being pulled into the wall, like an escalator. The plinth, which was at the base of the bridge, was retracting! His visor was still down, it magnified his plight. The other end of the bridge was being pulled away, and a gap was slowly forming. In a few moments, it would be a long drop with no bridge to stand on. Drake didn't think anymore and started to run!

Chapter 17: Meet the Dot

Drake could physically see the edge of the smoked glass, slowly retracting from the other building. This made him forget about the devastating height and made him focus. He was running at the fastest pace he could. He could make it–he could make it, he kept telling himself. There were no handrails or any form of safety on the narrow base. This was a health and safety nightmare. The gap was getting wider by the second and Drake didn't know if he really could make it.

Come on, he willed himself on. It hadn't taken him long to run three quarters of the way across this crazy platform. But the distance from the end of the bridge to the other side was almost two metres. He couldn't stop now-he had to make it. Drake pushed on and without thinking, he lurched forward. In his heart, he knew he wasn't going to make it. It was just too far, but the wind gave him a little more lift.

'Aargh…' he squealed as his whole world collapsed in that moment. He almost fell and expected to tumble like a rag doll down the side of the building. He was only in the air for a split-second and ended up flat on his face! He'd been travelling at such a speed that when he leapt off, the momentum carried him on with the wind as a cushion. He found himself sliding across a glass floor and straight through the opening on the other side. In the small amount of time he had to protect himself, Drake covered his head as best as he could.

Thud! The impact was minimal and without thinking, he got to his feet. There was a well-lit stairwell and a downward spiral of steps. He checked his watch and saw the dot still wasn't too far away. He could soon catch up and end this nightmare. The time, what was the time? Four minutes, that's all he had left. He knew that would be it. He dashed downwards, in a frenzy of legs and arms. He burst downwards and overbalanced, rubbing his shoulder against the smooth painted walls. He could hear shuffling feet; hurried footsteps were not too far below. This gave him more intensity. The Master was within range; the excitement was too heavy to bear.

'I'm coming dot baby,' he called out, his thin voice echoing through the chamber. He was moving so fast that the steps became a blur. Round and round he went-down and down. He felt giddy and sick but kept going.

'Oh my God,' he gasped, 'I can see him.' Through the centre of the staircase, he could see an elbow and a foot. The dot was only two floors below and Drake was catching him up. He couldn't believe it. He was hot and sweaty, his lungs felt as though they were going to explode. He was breathless and excited at the same time. The palms of his hands were moist and when he reached out to steady himself, he slid forward on the smooth painted surface and surged forward.

He was going too fast and tumbled down the last flight, luckily for him there wasn't far to fall. Drake fell out of the stairwell and into a corridor. As he hit the floor, he could see his target opening a door and disappearing inside. Battered and bruised, Drake got unsteadily to his feet again. He didn't have time to check his injuries or any aches. He just had to touch this idiot and escape this madness. Still feeling dizzy and unsure of his steps, he scrambled his way to the door and flung himself inside.

It was dark yet again, and he was getting used to the situation. But he landed on a soft surface. It felt more like a bench or sofa. Where was the dot, though? It was too dark to see anything except his watch. Two minutes to go, his heart sank, but the dot was only a couple of metres away. Then there was a jerk and whatever he was sitting on moved! He was confused. The next thing he heard was the clunk-clunk-clunk of metal rolling over metal.

'Where the hell am I?' he cursed. But this sensation felt familiar somehow. Whatever he was sitting in tilted from side to side. Drake reached out in the darkness and felt a steel bar at his fingertips. This was so familiar to him.

'This is either a ghost train or a rollercoaster,' he presumed, 'I don't believe this.' It was the only reasonable explanation he could think of. The momentum picked up, and it felt more and more like a ride of some sort. Suddenly the car began to climb and shunted violently, heaving Drake forward and back. There was also no strap or seatbelt to hold him in. Then light filtered in from somewhere and this made everything feel more real. Now things were getting strange. He *was* on a rollercoaster. He looked around and realised he was sitting in the middle of a string of cars. This was one of the old-fashioned rollercoasters from a funfair. Drake could see that four carriages ahead, someone was sitting alone at the front.

'Oh my God, it's the dot. The Master!' he could see the back of his head. He wasn't moving a muscle. A side wind whipped at his inky black hair, ruffling his thick locks. He looked familiar somehow.

The track was fully visible now. The ride was climbing up to a huge peak. He knew what he had to do, and it scared him silly. He'd seen it done in countless movies, but this time it was his turn. He knew he had to climb out while this thing was moving! This was the only way he could touch the dot. There were only four cars between them, and the master was just up ahead; there was nowhere for him to go! Drake had him at last.

He had to be quick, before the ride climbed too high and got too fast, and before the time ran out. Drake didn't have time to think; he climbed over and tumbled into the next car. He righted himself and could see the person ahead so much clearer. But he wasn't moving, why? To his utter horror, Drake realised that he was almost out of time. The rollercoaster was about to plummet over the loop. He lurched forward and clambered into the next car and then quickly into the next one. There was only one carriage between them, and he had to strike immediately. Aching and bloodied, Drake slumped into the car just behind the dot. He got to his knees just as they entered the drop. Drake fell forward, and the dot suddenly turned to meet him.

'Oh my God,' Drake uttered and couldn't speak anymore. The dot was him; his own eyes were peering back at him. Hold on, it was Crystal–no wait a minute, it was Scott–now it was Mike Bevan, the game shop owner! The wind blasted his face as the cars slowly descended. The image reached out to touch him... their fingertips connected, and the watch stopped at zero!

Chapter 18: Funfair

Icy cold droplets of water stung his nose and cheeks, forcing Drake to open his eyes. He shook his head vigorously and sat up. He was woozy, and it took a while for everything to stop spinning. The fine rain soaked his clothes and dripped off his nose. He wiped the excess water from his face and looked around. Where was he now? He seemed to have asked himself that question all the way through.

He was sitting at the base of an old abandoned rollercoaster ride in what looked like a long-forgotten funfair. It was familiar somehow, but obviously couldn't be.

'Is this another trick of the game?' Drake asked himself. It didn't feel as if it was an illusion, but tricks were there to fool the mind, so he tried to keep a clear head. He remembered the timer and quickly reacted by raising his arm to check his watch. It wasn't there! He stared at his arm in disbelief; he wasn't wearing his jumpsuit either. What was going on? He was sitting in his normal clothes. The ones he'd been wearing before getting sucked into the game.

'Am I out?' He said the words, but they didn't register at first. 'If I am out, then where exactly am I?' He shivered as the rain seeped through the material, to his skin. 'I'm in my normal clothes, I'm cold and the air feels different. I must be out of Death Trap.' An enormous smile sprang to his face.

Drake leaned forward to get to his feet, and that's when the pain took over.

'Aaaargh,' he groaned. Everything from his neck down hurt. He tried again, but this time gave his limbs more time to respond. It still hurt, but was manageable. Climbing to his feet, Drake felt every ache like an old man. Once fully up, he stretched his back. It felt good. He wiped away the excess water from his face again. His hair was soaked, and the thick strands dripped rain like a drainpipe.

He recognised nothing, so why did it feel like he did? Then he recalled what his mother had told him earlier, much earlier before the game. Huntsville had a funfair at one time, many years ago, she'd said. This has got to be the old fair on the outskirts of the town, he reasoned.

Suddenly, a dog appeared out of nowhere and went sniffing around the steps just below where he stood. It looked up at him and started barking. Drake stared back at the dog.

'Sheppy boy, what are you up to?' The voice of his owner echoed the open landscape. He saw Drake and eased up, a look of uncertainty and fear etched across his lined face.

'Come *here* boy, we've got to go,' the owner called nervously. The dog did as he was ordered and made his way to his master's side. He turned and growled at Drake, baring his teeth. This gave the old man a slight lift of confidence.

'It's OK mister,' Drake called back sensing the man's hesitation. 'I wouldn't hurt him, honest,' he said innocently. The man paused for a moment, not knowing how to respond.

'What are you doing out here, son? You looked soaked,' the old man asked. He was wearing a raincoat with a baseball cap. His dog Sheppy was also wearing rain protection.

'I'm new here. I've been walking and got lost. I need to find the way back to Huntsville,' Drake lied. The dog kept on growling.

'Oh, well, that's no problem,' his demeanour softened. 'Sheppy, stop it.' The dog was persistent. 'Sheppy, I said shush,' the man said with a grunt. The dog gave a groan and stopped. 'Just follow that road and it'll take you into town. Only about ten minutes or so,' he said, pointing towards a line of streetlights outside the compound. Drake flicked his head in the direction and back to the man.

'Thanks,' Drake replied and nodded as he walked away. He left them behind and followed the instructions he was given. The rain brought with it blackened clouds that dimmed the already overcast sky. Drake thought to himself, what seemed like days inside the game must have only been an hour and fifteen minutes. He still found it hard to believe he was out, and the adventure he'd taken was over.

The rain didn't persist and started easing off. It must have been raining a while, he pondered; the road and pavement each side glistened like glass under the brightening sky.

It took roughly the ten minutes the guy had said it would, to reach the town. But it was an uncomfortable walk. The creases in his damp jeans cut into his inner thighs and the back of his knees. He so wanted to get home and rip off his wet clothing. He knew his mum would freak, but he could handle that. Drake cut across the main road. At this distance, he could see some of the brightly lit shops in the town and other's that were dimmer. The gaming arcade came into view, and that gave him a shudder. The thought of what he'd just gone through was still fresh in his mind. It had only just happened, hadn't it?

'Mike Bevan, the Master,' he said.

People were milling around, making their way to the car park. The shops were just about to close. It must be half-past five, he thought.

He knew the game shop would be open until seven, but he wanted to avoid it tonight. He'd had enough of that place for one day and mum would have dinner ready by six. He was about to cross the road to avoid the shop altogether when he noticed a different colour poster in the window. He was keen to know what was new to the gaming world, so he wandered over. There was a puddle on the pavement directly outside, reflecting the bright, fluorescent colours of the display. Mike always put a poster of the new games on a luminous background, to give it maximum exposure. It had been a good ploy in the past because it always caught Drake's attention. This was a new game he hadn't seen before. Drake drifted nearer.

In the half-light, he could just make out what the

poster depicted. It revealed a figure of someone running away into the distance. Drake leaned in closer, trying not to step into the puddle; he was wet enough already. He saw the full theme. The silhouette in the frame resembled a teenager of about his stature. It appeared to be escaping from a tall-darkened villain in the foreground. The game was a simple race and chase. The title was genius and simple too. Hunted: there is no escape!

He thought about checking it out and stepped back with total indecision. He mulled it over for a moment and stopped–what was he thinking? He couldn't risk it–he'd had enough.

Drake made up his mind, there and then. And as he walked in the direction of his home–he decided life was going to be different from now on. But the curiosity of that gaming arcade was always going to haunt him.

THE END

www.ingramcontent.com/pod-product-compliance
Lightning Source LLC
Chambersburg PA
CBHW010400310726
48979CB00017B/2794/J

* 9 7 8 1 9 1 2 9 4 8 2 2 2 *